Pigeon House

PIGEON HOUSE

Shilo Niziolek

Querencia Press – Chicago IL

QUERENCIA PRESS

ISBN 978 1 959118 96 1

.

www.querenciapress.com

First Published in 2024

Querencia Press, LLC
Chicago IL

Printed & Bound in the United States of America

"What sort of world would it be if people bled all over the sidewalks, if they wept under trees, smacked whomever they despised, kissed strangers, revealed themselves?"

—Alice Hoffman, *The Ice Queen*

CONTENTS

Torpedo

I watched the flaming trees of autumn bristle as we passed by them on the bus. A man got on, shoulders held taut, a light kick in his step, like he might take off and fly. It was you, but I didn't think you saw me, so I hunkered down in my seat, pulling my hoodie over my wind-blown hair.

Just yesterday, as I dipped my french fries into my frosty, the salt burning the paper cut on my finger, you came barreling around the corner on the street. Again, you didn't see me, but I stared blankly, slurping the ice cream off each individual finger.

After you and the bus were gone, I saw a woman with your chin. There was a dent in it that gave it a bit of a hook. I wanted to march right up to her, twist her chin in the palm of my hand, bring her face to mine, but I sat there, blatantly staring. It was only when her eyes met mine that I discovered she wasn't you. She narrowed her eyes into olive slits, frowned, the crease in her chin growing broader.

My therapist said that I am manifesting you, that my obsession with you is clouding my ability to reason, but I think I can still see reason well enough. When I see a man walk with a kick in his step, back facing me, it is you walking away. Every freckled constellation on someone's skin is the view of your arms encasing me.

I can't tell anyone else what I've been seeing.

There, the flash of your blue eyes simmering to black.

Sometimes I don't even believe me.

If I still talked to our old friends they'd say, "That's not him, Jenny. That's a different man. Can't you see, the stoop of his shoulders, too exaggerated. His hands not clenched tightly enough. No cigarette in hand. No half-raised smile. No quirk of the lip."

As if it were so easy, as if I can extract the dream of him, pry the pressure of his lips from my skin, his skin from under my fingernails, his words tucked under the tissue, the mesh wiring of a promised eternity.

I walk across the cool green of the bridge, steeples pressing up into fog and darkness. I hear the steps behind me. I hear them alright. They sound a bit like a heartbeat. There's thunder above me, thunder below. Car lights fracture through the misty air and I feel a trundling in my ears.

The last thing he'll see is my silhouette plummeting. A red sweatshirt dashing to the ground. And when they pull me from the river, my face will be bloated with memory.

And when he goes to his lover on the bed, he thinks, only for a moment, that there I am in the lift of her long eyelashes. A flash, and the image of me overlays on top of her, my body curled naked on his sheets, my body calling.

He'll remember the words he said, they'll ricochet like the drum of a bell.

And, later, there I'll be, the sway in my hips of a woman crossing the intersection. And there, again, me, in the childish wonder of a seven-year-old girl, fondling the pointed dahlia petals. When he turns around: the sensation of me creeping up his neck.

Months later he'll go to his lover, "Someone's following me," he'll say.

From inside her face, I'll smile out at him.

River Tide

She stood under the maple and watched the butter yellow leaves drift to the ground. The maple was always the first to begin losing its leaves when the winds changed. Her toes, bare and unpainted, pressed into the moss. Looking down, she was startled by the contrast of mud pressed up, already drying, around the bright pink skin of her cold toes. *How long had she been standing there?* She couldn't be sure. Below, the hillside was lined with old Victorian houses. Historic Society plaques kept polished by the rain were displayed on the side of their paneling and gates. A conglomerate of pastel purples, pinks, blues, and greens looked up at her. A town full of rows and rows of box-shaped, people-inhabited, macarons.

The wind kicked up and the Columbia River below frothed and rioted against the river walk. People made their way along the black tar path snaking the river's edge. They stopped every few yards, looking out at the unrelenting tide, the unforgiveable mouth of the beautiful beast. A grey bank of fog broiled around the Easter-egg green pillars of the Megler bridge, and Washington played its long-standing game of hide-and-seek. Peeking out across the expanse, disappearing, peeking out, disappearing, lost momentarily in its thick coat of clouds.

She couldn't remember the last time she had crossed that bridge. It served as a grounding reminder that she was there, alive, body cold and compressed inside its illness. Once, the bridge had served as a gateway. She could momentarily escape across it, to the place the locals called Never-Never-Land, a cove just across the river, a bunker to crouch down in, to smoke in, to kiss in, to carve your names in the weathered cement, to look across into Astoria, standing tall and impending, vibrating with sweet green life.

Why had she come outside? When? It had been at least two months since she had stepped out her own door. A delivery service delivered food. She didn't need much anymore. Just some tea and some toast. The illness was coming swift and loud now. Food and drink couldn't quench her thirst. *The crows. That must have been it.* She wanted to see the crows swirling in the brewing storm. Black ink across sky. They had been calling. Rioting. From inside the house the old lace-trimmed eaves hung over the edge of the roof, blocking her view. She had broken the seal of the back door, released with crisp exhaustion, like coming up out of deep water for air. Once, she had jumped off the Alderbrook Bridge into the swaying tide and her feet had squished down deep into the quicksand of river mud, trying to seal her body into the tomb of the grey-green water. The dahlias were still out in their late bloom, colors fading at the edge of the petals, and when she stepped off the porch into their delicate scent she had nearly been bent backwards in grief. Disoriented, she set out into the damp lawn. She looked up just in time to witness the crows catapult from view, off into the edge of her portion of the sky.

Whoosh, the air called around her.

The dry creases of her mouth peeled apart in wonder.

"Goodbye!" she yelled. Her voice came out foreign, thick and raspy on her tongue.

Now, a slow gentle mist makes its way up from the river, dancing through the rows of macaron houses, and kisses her lightly, first her lips, then one by one the lids of her closed eyes.

Suddenly, breathless, she lifts a shaking hand up and touches the side of her cheek, her eyes pressed tightly shut at something briefly remembered. Was it the touch of a man? A rough and tender touch as he laid her body down, down, down, in the soil, wearing a blanket of ferns and moss and damp pine needles. Or another moment? A mother rocking her child to sleep, hands scented with the smell of cotton. An old country song her mother used to sing, *As I went down to the river to pray...*

A branch snaps and her eyes open, burning with a recollection of heat. Unblinking, she sees chestnut eyes stare at her, frozen only a few feet away. The doe's blink goes unanswered. Its front hoof, held mid-step, comes down slowly. Its fur glistens with the condensation of river rain, the heavy mist that seems to never stop falling all around and inside them: on the bright red and white caps of death poking heads up and out and around the forest floor, on the stoops of the porches lining the streets, settling into the cracks and crevices, turning itself into a devouring and unending mold.

The doe takes one step. And then another.

She comes closer. Close enough to touch. She blinks at the doe. The doe, another step. She lifts her hand, trembling slightly, held out, cupped, but not daring to be the first to touch. The doe leans her head briefly against her hand. The doe's eyes close loosely, as if on the way to sleep. The fur, soft and coarse at once, on her fingertips. A maple leaf the size of a woman's hand drifts down between them, landing on the center of the deer's head. She jerks her head in response, and just as quickly as she appeared, bounds swiftly away, up and over the rose bush, past the rhododendron. Her hooves click and clatter on the black tar. Two more bounds and she evaporates into the cover of the Douglas fir and cedarwood, up the hill where fog descends quickly, shifting in the first moments of dusk.

The world silences around her. Hand still out, reaching, a tingle of memory upon it, she takes one step toward the woods, imagining that she could become a deer, that she could disappear in the dark of the woods. That the woods, too, would come to meet her, collect her on the spot where life ends and begins again.

***

Her body, lithe, curled in on itself. A boy. Red-brown hair walks away from her in the woods. Words tied up and hung cruelly, carelessly in the air, pinned to the barks of the trees. Her black pants, her pale green sweater. Her knees hit the soft ground, sinking in. A slow, tepid rocking. A motion. A stillness. Tears, red hot and blistering. Hands pressing down, fingers digging into mud. A wail, a sound, so close to her, deep inside and outside of her. Red lips swollen from the force of their needy kisses shared only minutes before in the front seat of her car. Back pressed roughly up against the car door, the handle pressing uncomfortably against her spine.

The sound emitting from her ricochets off every surface. It silences the birds. It springs forth with such force she is unaware of the seeping warmth.

***

No one would ever know how heavy and damp grief could be unless they cried so forcefully that they wet themselves. Even later, years later, she would think how interesting, that grief could become a dried-out thing, a husk of skin. Then, there were hands lifting her up off her knees. There was red-brown hair, a freckled face, cool blue eyes staring in earnest. There was a kiss. There was skin and clothes soaked from the rain and her own body's loss. Wild abandon.

Then, again, here she was. A body frail. A body tight. A body forgotten.

The deer long gone.

The crows somewhere else, in someone else's trees, swooping down to collect shining, blinding objects, one after the other. A quick succession of hopes.

Her hand raised to her throat, touched the place where the swelling had begun. Now, just a line, a body sewn shut. Hidden underneath was what they could not get.

***

"Too aggressive," the doctor said.

"I am unforgiving," she said. "Makes sense that my cancer would be too."

The doctor, unsure of his response, of the void, lifted a cheek, a half-undeceiving, *I'm sorry you are going to die, that we are all going to die, that we are dying,* acknowledgement.

"I know a nice hospice nurse," he offered. "We can make you as comfortable as possible."

"I never wanted comfort," she said before shaking the doctor's hand and walking away.

***

It was startling, the way time moved without any empathy, without consequence.

A light in an upstairs window illuminated a bedroom two houses over. The dusting of water continued, perpetual motion. A woman pulled a maroon sweater over her head in the window above, revealing a desert sand colored bra and her arms, muscled and thorough in their ability to hold a body up when need be. She watched the woman looking down at the purple clouds coalescing on the horizon, endlessly reaching out to the sea she knew was there in the distant horizon. The woman wrapped her arms tight around her chest, then, slowly, moved them down, rubbing her small stomach, barely showing a swelling of the future in the hollow of her belly.

She almost cried out in wonder. In pain. She reached down, touched her empty belly, her stomach flat from illness. She imagined a changing. A growing. She felt the turn. A rolling over. An ache inside her skin wrapped around another. A skin inside a skin. A heart inside, beating, up against the thick red breadth of another heart.

***

She felt her mother's hands on the protrusion of her stomach, "Hello, my sweet girl. My baby's baby. Hello, angel."

***

The woman in the window turned away, unclasped her bra in one quick motion, let it slide from her shoulders, then moved from view. She looked down at the river, rapids picking up steam, moving in ripples down the surface, foam rising, breaking, releasing back into the blue-green-black, gathering at the edges, slamming against edges.

***

A cry of pain. Her body seeped red on the floor around her as she lost her child. The rain fell in long gray slats. The man she wished she didn't love kept calling, screaming, howling on her answering machine.

"Why would you do this to me?" he screeched, blaming her, as if she had wanted this, as if she had prayed for the death of her child and brought it into fruition with the weight of her own desire, the same way he felt drawn to her again and again, despite all the times he ran away.

He had already lost two children. One, taken from him by the mother, doing what was best for her child, taking her son away from a man that acted like a demon after the child's first breath. The second, taken away by something else, a deep sadness, a coil roped around its neck on exit. A breath never taken. Its birth a death. The third, lost.

The phone went unanswered. It went unanswered. Its wires unplugged.

***

The sound of sea lions calling up from the East Mooring Basin reverberated around her, broke the memory into bits. They sprinkled out and around her, fell on the fuzzy lips of the ferns. She never could imagine what the sea lions were saying. It could be anger causing them to cry out. It could be some form of song. She looked down at her body, found herself sitting on the rickety old bench against the ivy that oozed around everything: the trunks of the trees, the staircase, around and about the house with its daisy yellow pallets, hidden by deep leafy green. The white paint of the bench flaked off when she reached down to touch it. Paint particles specked the skin of her freezing, bright red hands.

Her mom, when they'd first moved to this island of a town, sat on a hill that might have reached up to touch the gods if the gods hadn't forsaken them long ago. Her mom, down on her knees, sanding by hand the white paint off the original hardwoods of their new-old home. Sixteen, knees fiery bright from kneeling and crawling, making their way slowly across each inch of the floors.

"Why can't we use an electric sander," she asked, exasperated.

Her mom, "The back-breaking work of life is best done with your own two hands."

***

Months after her miscarriage, her mom arrived with cleaning supplies. Down on her knees in the upstairs bathroom she sat scrubbing, scrubbing, scrubbing the bloody tide out of the tub. Nails bleached crimson for days after.

***

Her mom rocked in her chair in her childhood home, a book in one hand, her daughter's body curled and cocooned in the other. The bunnies on the page of *Peter Rabbit* peered up at them from outside the grove. Her mother's voice lifted out of her, "They lived with their Mother in a sand-bank, underneath the root of a very big fir-tree."

***

Her mother's voice.

When she died two years ago, after a horrific and unexpected stroke, her mother's voice rising up around her in the dark of the night, in a sleep or a non-sleep half-sleep, her silhouette sitting on the edge of her bed, quoting books again, "I'll love you forever. I'll like you for always."

***

A white and brown speckled rabbit darted out from behind a tree and disappeared just as quickly around the side of the house. The sea lions trumpeted below. The crows moved across the sky, back into view, cackling all the while. The river rushed in, pulled out, rushed in. The fog crept up around the macaron houses. The Megler Bridge disappeared completely, only to reappear moments later; a lady trapped in an endless game of chase. Somewhere nearby a door slammed. A fruit fell from a crab apple tree in the neighbor's yard, landing with a thud before rolling downhill. A dog barked in the distance.

She stood.

The moss and mud squished between her toes. The smell of salt and fir filled the air. She turned from the world, pulled her dark green sweater tightly around her body, and made her way, step by step, down the cool sidewalk of the hill. The river called to her. It wanted to touch her body, lap at her toes.

Edging the small bank behind the Maritime Museum, she heard the jangle of the trolley trundling down the tracks. Two children swung from branches on a nearby tree. The sounds of water lightly thudding against the rocks and the bank and her ankles rocked her like the gentlest lullaby. A peel of laughter drifted from down the street.

A blue heron lifted off from a pillar and sailed down the snake of the river and out of sight.

Sanctuary

It began with cracks in the glass. Miniature pine trees began sprouting from the screen. The cracks turned into roots and the roots into trunks and the trunks into trees.

I took the phone to my cellular provider.

"What do you make of this?" I asked. The tech was wearing a bright orange sweater vest.

He barely looked up from his tablet. "It appears," he paused, "that your phone is growing trees." He tossed my phone into the trash and handed me a replacement.

I held my new glossy screen in the palm of my hand, happy to again find the right angles in place, the keys usable, my peach complexion reflecting off the glass of the screen. I glanced at the trash bin on my way out the door. The tips of the pines were just beginning to peer over the edge.

On my walk home through the steel labyrinth of the city I thought I felt a tree following me home in the mirrored buildings. Each time I turned around there were only people, heads down, the light from their phones streaming onto their sallow cheeks, shadows walking.

I entered my apartment and draped myself over the bed, pleased to see that unsightly greenery had not again sprouted from my phone. The charcoal walls reflected nothing back at me.

For hours I scrolled and scrolled and scrolled, the light shifting from yellow to pink to night. I fell asleep with my phone in my hand. I awoke to the sensation of a thousand little slivers protruding from my hands. Stumbling to the bathroom, I clicked on the unnatural light. In my palm where my phone had slept grew a tiny bonsai, the roots raising clean from my skin. A kraken in the night.

Sitting down on the cool porcelain ridge of my bathtub, I watched as the wiry branches crept out.

"There is no sunshine for you here," I heard myself say.

My eyes felt pushed back in my skull, as if looking at my own body from a great distance.

This isn't happening.

I shook my head, bringing myself back into my body.

I'd heard of cases like this, but I was determined not to let it happen to me. *I barely even use my phone*, I thought, reaching for the tweezers behind the porcelain sink. I pried each root, one by one, from the lining of my skin and flushed the bonsai down the toilet. My skin closed back up, unmarred. When I clicked off the light, I followed the faint glow of the streetlight illuminating my steps to the bed. I felt my arms begin to itch, as if fire ants tunneled into my bones. By the light of my phone, I saw the yellow creep of aspen leaves, littering what should have been my lightly freckled skin, making a home.

I grabbed my phone and keys, slipped on shoes and covered myself in my afghan, wincing at the pain as it stretched over the miniature trees.

I hailed a cab but when the light from the street shone on me, he said, "I'm sorry. I can't help you." Looking down, I saw what he saw. Bright yellow leaves, tendrils really, stretching out at the edges of the afghan, pushing through the openings of my grandmother's yarn.

He sped away, as if I was contagious. A mossy virus under rising sun.

I ran the twenty blocks to the closest emergency room, but by the time I arrived miniature elms had taken away my opposable thumbs. Standing outside the sliding doors I asked google, "How fast do elm trees grow?"

A robotic voice replied, "The American Elm grows fast in any environment."

I groaned before stepping through the open doors.

I crossed to the front desk, let out a hiccup, and a gum tree sapling peeled out from the top of my head. Little, green, spikey gum balls hung at the ends of my short blond hair like beads or snake heads on a marble statue.

The woman at the front desk took one look at me, opened the swinging white doors, and bellowed, "We've got another grower out here!"

An entourage of medical staff came filtering through the doors, ushering me back outside the hospital as quickly as possible. One with a giant pair of sheers trimmed the trees from my arms, head, and thumbs. The trees planted symmetrically in perfectly manicured squares of grass between slabs of sidewalk all seemed to shimmy their leaves with each cut, as if in collective pain. A quiet protest that I felt attuned to, like the rattling of the leaves was happening somewhere in the depths of my chest. A man in a green doctor's mask yelled for someone to call the bus and a bright yellow school bus came screeching around the corner.

"What is happening to me?" I whispered through the cacophony around me.

A female doctor with kind eyes took my hand, momentarily empty of trees. "Unfortunately, once it starts it can't be reversed. There is no cure. The more we chop them down the faster they grow, but we are going to take you to a sanctuary. A place to rest." Tears welled and fell. I looked down to the sound of tiny pinecones bouncing off the pavement and rolling into the street.

My hand pulled from hers as I was lifted onto the bus by large sturdy hands. When I turned to look the man in the eyes, he averted his gaze. Was he ashamed he couldn't do more for me? Imagining what the roots looked like underneath my clothes? I stumbled on the steps of the bus, found it full of others in various stages of growth.

There was a teenage boy, red maple leaves unfurling from his ears and next to him a toddler whose face was coated in a thick layer of moss, building up the more she wept. Outside the toddler's window, a woman with long brown hair stooped, her shoulders bent into the arm of an orderly as they shook.

"I just," she choked, "the tablet helped keep him busy. I was just so tired." She wailed and the toddler, stiff with bark, couldn't turn his body to take one last look.

The last three rows of seats had been removed to make way for what used to be a large burly man. Where his face had been was now a Douglas fir, only a golden-red beard and drowsily blinking blue eyes remained. No lips for me to kiss if I wished it.

I sat down in an empty seat. I felt my legs melding together. The trunks of my tree getting heavier with each corner we took as we sped away, our bulk making the bus list to the left.

Only a twenty-minute drive outside the city and we came across rows and rows of sun dappled hills, a stream running through the curves of it.

I had to be carried off the bus by orderlies. On the short drive, the gum tree had grown back, taken root in my skull. My legs bound themselves to one another, my lips turned to a grainy bark. Spiky gum balls sprouted lime-green from my skin.

They placed each of us in nice rows along the stream bed, soaking up the water. My arms turned to branches as the day stretched out its limbs into night. When I awoke in the morning, a pile of my clothes lay shredded next to me, my shoes to the left and right, looked as if they had small bombs placed inside them and were ripped from front to back. By noon, another bus arrived and a small orderly went around with a trash bag, collecting our discarded material items. I felt nothing. I didn't need them anymore. I stretched my body toward the sunlight as it set at the west. I could feel my roots burrowing deeper into the ground, searching out mystery below me, the depths of which I couldn't have fathomed before. I felt a glimmer of the desire to know deeper, but it drifted away into the night.

We've been here awhile now. There are no screens left to scroll, memes to be liked, shows to binge. Only the endless scroll of sky, so many watercolor moods to binge, invisible heart emojis floating around our treetops.

Yesterday they brought a man. He looked like someone I might have loved. They laid him at the base of my body, bright red and white mushrooms popped out of the lining of his skin. Already he is more moss than man. The mushrooms spread, unfurl across my trunk. *Now this is what I call making love*, I thought before my mind drifted off, buoyed by the frequency of the wind.

After I Left

I changed my phone number, then took a coffee and a pack of cigarettes into the shower. I laid back, the porcelain chilling my skin and let the hot white heat pound and swelter around me. I counted the bruises on my skin, one for each time you said you loved me. The cat mewled at the door for what felt like hours. The heat turned tepid, then to ice.

I put a cap in the drain and watched the ashes float.

The next day I went down to the docks. Sitting on the edge, kicking my legs, I thought about calling you. The fog filtered down the river, enveloping the fishing vessels bobbing with the tide.

In my mind I watched a movement unfold. Saw myself from your body as I entered a room, leaned on the doorframe. My hair was curled, wound up on the top of my head in some fashionable, girl-who-runs-through-grass-fields style that I've never been able to replicate. My tank-top was lace white. Your hands lay open, palms up toward me, as if they were doing the talking. *What can I say?* They seemed to motion.

And when I smiled at you your voice cracked hello like a lighthouse searching.

PORCELAIN GHOSTS

-1-

I was born with violence in my bones and my teeth were the first to know it. As soon as they started pushing through my gums I began biting. They called me *Little Monster*. I think I've always been sick. I look like something that could eat a man. Last night I couldn't sleep. My roommate sat on the edge of my bed in her work dress, pastel pink and looking like someone from an old diner. She didn't know how to devour a man; she'd never even tried. You're either born with it or you're not; her canines never grew in. "Sometimes it makes me angry that I fell in love with someone who is so much like me," she said. "We're tiny baby narcissists searching for mirrors," I said, twisting the end of her long black braid around my pointer finger. I nodded to the mirror on my nightstand, tilted part way towards the bed, then got up and padded to the bathroom. Two black spiders ran in, one after the other, I tore up the tiles trying to find them. Squished them, one by one, with the imprint of my big toe. At night I check on my roommate, crack her door and watch her while she sleeps. She'll never know what bad love can do to a woman. When wasps crawl up my arms, I think about eating them. Sometimes I dream that all my teeth fall out of my mouth at once. When I had braces, they would all be attached, little train tracks littering the ground.

-2-

I still want all your ghosts. When I think of rivers rising into the sky, ready to swallow us all, I imagine standing naked, arms held open. In the end my reflection's not who I thought it was, and crows follow me wherever I go. I can't ask my mom if my biological father beat her while I was in the womb—even though I know he did during the short time she stayed with him after. You'd be surprised to know that the anger comes from my mom's side of the family. It's the intelligent madness. I've had enough of that. I like my body best when it is propelling through space, when I'm all bite and bark. I don't want to be humble; I want to be ferocious. I'm watching leaves rustle in the wind and clouds drift across the sky. There's so much peace inside the violence of a woman's body. My dog once caught a mouse and killed it with one clamped motion. It was screeching and then it was dead. She shook her head violently from side to side, wringing it out.

-3-

There was a ghost story my mom used to tell. In an old house that didn't yet have modern plumbing, lived my mother's family. Each September they heard the wailing of the parents whose eleven-year-old daughter had died while they lived there. All month long the parents cried, but they would never get their daughter back. She was bound to the land where she died. When you're a ghost, your body doesn't need the things it did before. She only thought she wanted to be real, forgot she could move through walls. I forgot to think about all the things an eleven-year-old would never have. Every September my mom would find the ghost girl sitting in the outhouse, crying into her empty hands.

-4-

There's damage in naming things. I don't name the things I want for fear of getting them. I wander the lonely streets. In my dreams it's a separate world and ghosts aren't ghosts, they are only the people I keep locked in a box, and a box isn't a box, it's my heart, and my heart isn't my own after all. I stepped out to the woods behind my backyard and found a note waiting for me. I followed a trail that wasn't where I left it and left a trail of teeth behind me, to guide me back home. My translucent feet left no marks on the ground, and each tooth I dropped began burrowing, stretching its roots down where I walked. There was a woman at the end of the trail where a waterfall met a river and I followed her body like water into the stream. We dove under, faced each other in the cool black rapids, eyes wide open, hair wrapped around my body—a straitjacket. Her lips formed sounds that echoed through me, "You're a ghost and you don't even know it. You're a hungry ghost, but a ghost all the same." She swam closer, her body fit around me. Into my ear, she spoke, "I'll pretend I never knew your name."

-5-

The first man I pretended to love had long chocolate hair that fell down his face in ringlets. We were young and I didn't have to try hard. I just swung my hips when I walked, sometimes hearing the click of my hip pop in and out. I felt satisfyingly sexual. I bought a pair of jeans that were laced up the sides with leather straps and when I danced in the dark of a school dance the boys stood in a row and watched me, mouths gaped. "Where'd you learn to move like that?" they asked. Do you know what it's like, realizing you've been a spider all along? I see the ghost of my former self dancing all around. When the boys I pretended to love think of me, I hope they think of my body, a lithe animal, a body twisting, filled with the temptation of wild bones.

-6-

I was born with violence in my bones and it shakes like the hollow branches of the cherry tree. A man once told me a ghost story. It went a little something like this: In the night I can still find you. I'll follow you across the land. Do you think you can run from me? That you can hide? When you dive from this car and hide in a ditch, I'll drive up the mountainside calling your name. I'm there watching. You may lay in bed beside another, but when you sleep, you'll dream of me. He told me this ghost story so many times, that when I try to conjure up other men, their breath turns to ice, and their lips are always the same. "Do you understand? You can never truly leave me," he said, the imprints of his fingers, pale ghosts under my skin.

-7-

I still want all your ghosts, and the sunflowers cast their petals as I walk by. I sneak into my roommates' room as she sleeps. With a serrated kitchen knife, I cut off her long black braid. I twine it through the yellow rose bush in the backyard, waiting for her to say something. When she comes out of the bathroom in the morning the cut looks as if she had it professionally done. A cute bob that frames her delicate features perfectly. "Have you seen my mustard yellow sweater," she asks, all rosy cheeks and eyelashes. I bite my tongue. I can't tell if she is playing coy. "It's hang-drying in my closet," I say. My teeth ache from the tight clench. A hornet comes in through the backdoor, drunk on weather. I shut it in the window and watch it, this way I can't be ignored or forgotten.

-*8*-

There was a ghost story my mom used to tell. The ghost didn't present herself to me, only to my mom and my sister. I'd lie if I said I wasn't a bit resentful. She wore a blue dress and kept her hair in long, blonde pigtails and lived in the yellow house next to the church. I never saw her, but I felt her all the same. If you were home alone sitting in the corner of the living room, a chill would surround you, and the front door would wobble on its latch. On many occasions the cats would go into a frenzy in the middle of the night, as if they sensed something I couldn't. One night, they launched themselves back and forth over my bed from one side to the other. I had nightmares about someone knocking at my window, and the desert winter wind howled its shrill cry. When I woke, I found three scratch marks on the outside of the glass. *Fingernails.* I can't be sure that the ghost wasn't me.

-9-

I only want what I can't have, that's why I stole my roommates' new boyfriend. I guess you could say, I borrowed him. It's not stealing if you give it back, used and unwashed. She doesn't know, but each time I watch him lean over to kiss her, I imagine his thin lips on my neck. When his hand is in hers, I feel the movement of his dry hands slip up my skirt. It was an accident, honest, but sometimes I turn into other people in the dark. At the bonfire she went off to go find somewhere to pee in the woods. She wanted me to go with her. "No, I'm too cold," I said, and wrapped her yellow scarf tighter around her neck, exposed to the cold without her plaited hair. But then I found myself being led to the opposite side of the fire, behind a tree. I listen to her go on and on about how great he is, what a good man, how he takes care of her, never pressures her, is delicate in bed. But let her think what she wants. His lips tasted like her watermelon chapstick. Even good men are not good men.

-10-

I know how to pretend to love a man.

1. Convince yourself you want out of whatever life you're living.
2. Kiss him slow and sweet.
3. Convince yourself that you could love him.
4. Pretend the ghost of the man you love isn't there beside you when you sleep.
5. Let the man think that you love him.
6. When he says I love you first, don't say it back immediately—but, eventually, say it back.
7. When he says, "move in with me," say, "okay."
8. Imagine that the man you love is outside your window.
9. Fuck him the way he asks to be fucked.
10. When you start crying, roll over and tell him nothing.
11. Think only, *one foot out the door.*
12. Pack up most of your belongings and begin to move out while he's out of town.
13. Don't be surprised when he keeps the boxes you didn't get to and lights them on fire, the tiny bones of porcelain dolls, ghosts evaporating into the cold December air.

-11-

I was born with violence in my bones, and when I lop the yellow rose bushes down, I cut the thorns from the stems and sew them into a necklace. *Rose teeth*, I think as they bite into my skin. I still want all your ghosts, so I go to the graveyard during a crescent moon and I collect the memorials left behind. My closet is filled with them, wilting flowers, vases and vases of them, love letters, stuffed and soaking teddy bears, each night I open the closet door and the stench of old haunts wafts out at me. *Ghost babies*, I think. There was a ghost story my mom used to tell. "There once was a blonde girl with lashes like caterpillars who carved out her own heart, the end." I know how to pretend to love a man, you just turn your body inside out. Bite down, bone on bone, when he undresses you. Nothing but a ghost.

The Blue

Jess stood on the edge of Little Crater Lake smoking his last cigarette. The glow from the tip was in front of his face but also in the blue mirror of the water. A tree, long enough to stretch across the small lake reached its tendril-like limbs under the surface. Long dead tree trunks littered the base, all visible through the glacial mountain water of Mt. Hood. It was late autumn, but the first snow hadn't fallen yet. It would soon, he could tell. The air had that tell-tale bite and the wind whistled around him.

He hunkered lower into his denim jacket, pulling up the collar to protect his cheeks from the chill. He ashed his cigarette one last time into the clear blue, then twisted it in tight circles onto the wood rail beam that overlooked the water, leaving a perfect black circle in the embers' wake.

Jess turned and sat on the wooden bench. It felt like ice crystals formed on his butt bones as soon as he sat, and a shiver ran through him like a shock of light.

He stared into the sheen of the lake and tried to conjure up her face, brown hair like liquid held back with a green bandana, standing on the edge of the mountain, turned toward him, waiting for him to catch up. That was the last time he had seen her smile. He wiped his face with his hands, erasing the image. He couldn't think about what came after that. Or he couldn't not think about it. The way she turned from him in the bed. The tightness in her ankles even in her sleep, poised to run. It wasn't something he did. It was all the things he didn't do. He didn't try to hold her close. Never reached for her hand. She was always there, leaning her weight against him, smiling up at his face, leaning in for a kiss. He didn't go to the picnic with her family that one sunny Saturday she asked. "Not for me," he said. She must have realized, at some point, that he couldn't give.

He could only take and take and take. He was gluttonous when it came to her. And now he'd never have his fill.

The wind howled and he stood and began to strip down, leaving a hasty pile of blue jeans and black jacket crumpled over his socks and boots in the mud. In his striped boxers he looked down at the white of his legs. Sickened, he dove headfirst into the water, arching up over the downed log. He sunk deeper, opening his eyes to the blue light that shone through him.

Eventually his body clamored for air and out he shot into the November mountain chill. He rolled to his back and trembled with the intense shock of the cold. Looking up at the grey sky, he watched first one lone flake flutter down and land on the water's surface, then another, until the snow catapulted all around, falling into the white of his body. He let out a howl that turned into a cry and drifted on the water into the opening of a moan. A chorus of sounds rose up around him, an infinity of animal clatter and hunger.

Jess was dying. He was freezing to death; he could feel it starting in his toes. They were no longer connected to his body; they weren't of the body they were of the water. He was becoming transparent, if not to the eye, then to his own heart. Soon, he knew, a rabbit or cougar would come by. They'd look out and they'd see his body turned to light, turned to crystalline blue weight, sunk to the bottom. A person could walk the edge of the lake, thinking it odd that what was normally clear was suddenly milky blue. He moved his fingers, pulled one hand out of the water and in front of his face. It was his body. The same body that had been beaten. Knuckles permanently swollen from the walls he had punched. The same body that had ran from his parent's home, slept under bridges, fingers that refused to call his mom, flipped off his dad, forgot his little sister. The same body Naomi had curled into, that he had curled around her in his sleep, unaware, only to wake and find his face buried in the smell of tea tree, like drinking a glass of rain.

He rolled to his stomach and began swimming to the edge, pulled himself from the lake. Taking deep galloping breaths, he grabbed his clothes and shoes from the ground, turned and sprinted through the field in the snow into the encroaching dark. He made his way to the dark green of his jeep, silhouetted in the night. He sat with the heater blasting until he could feel his toes, his knees, his penis, his belly button, his collarbone, his ears, his nose, watched as his fingers, tinged in blue, thawed. The moon lifted high in the sky and cast the fallen snow in a blinding light. He touched his hands to his face, discovering that he still existed. He wasn't a translucent ghost floating at the bottom of a clear blue lake. He laughed until his throat grew hoarse. Headlights bloomed around the bend of the parking lot. An older couple glanced in his window through theirs as they trundled by. The old man's mouth quirked up in some sacred form of recognition. Jess could not fathom to comprehend, but he felt a strange sort of nostalgia for the old man and his half smile the moment they passed. The snow hushed around him as the wheels of the couple's car crunched quietly back into the night. Slowly, he removed his damp boxers and put his clothes on one by one, his limbs still moving timidly. His fingers hesitant, brand new.

The Fisherman's Wife

She first appeared to him on the deck of his boat, *The Maria*. He was out fishing for salmon and went down into the cabin for his rain gear as a deep purple cloud moved off the ocean and over the Columbia River. He was sliding his legs into his Grundens when he felt the boat bow deeply on the back end.

"Oh no you don't," he called, rustling into his rain gear quicker, thinking a seal had tried to hop aboard to steal fish, as they are known to do.

He returned to the open air just as the rain moved across the water and came pelting down. There was no sign of a seal on the deck, so he turned to reel in his net, the rain turning quickly into a downpour. That's when he saw her, completely naked and crouched near the nets. She stared at him, a half-smile crossing her lips while the rain soaked the long, curly, brown hair that careened down and around her moon pale skin.

He stared back, mouth agape like a trout out of water, rain streaming down his face, before collecting his wits.

"What in the hell are you doing on my boat, girl! And where are your damn clothes?" he yelled over the squall, but she made no motion to reply.

He crossed the deck and grabbed her gently by the elbow, pulling her up.

"Well, come on now. Let's get you out of this rain."

He walked her down to the cabin, rustled around in a metal bin attached to the wall, and pulled out a rough old wool blanket that he wrapped around her body, tucking her in like a child, but this was no child and his gaze lingered on her bare shoulder. She wasn't trembling, barely seemed to register the cold at all, only watched him with an eerie silence and eyes black like spilled oil. He fumbled with his pack of cigarettes, unable to pull his eyes from her stare, and lit up a smoke, his own hands trembling.

He was no longer a young man—past the age where beauties such as this would pay him much attention—though he thought he was still handsome in that rugged and wild way that fishermen seem to retain, no matter their age, because of the nature of their time spent on the unruly water.

"What's your name?"

She didn't respond, only shook her head slightly from side to side and continued to stare at him openly, curiously.

The sound of the rain on the tin roof of the cabin sent shock waves through his body. And when she stood and dropped the blanket, crossing the small space between them, pulling down the suspenders of his rain pants, it was all he could do to remember to take the cigarette dangling from his bottom lip and put it out on the wall before he enveloped her, allowing her insatiable thirst to wash over him.

She never spoke one word, not one sound uttered, but her body moved like water—up, around, and under him. Her skin so soft it was as if she had stepped out of a bath of coconut oil. Her skin to his lips tasted like salt and he felt like a man in a dream. Afterwards, she was lulled to sleep by the rock of the boat, the storm had abated during their time and streams of sunlight shown wildly above. He pulled his arm from under her body, staring down at her, trying to memorize her form while he lit another cigarette and stepped out onto the deck barefooted. He'd forgotten to pull in the net and found it filled, rich with salmon. He laughed loudly to himself as he reeled it in. He felt like Lir himself, the Irish god of the sea. When he was done, he drove the boat back to Pier 39, the woman sleeping soundlessly on her side on the floor, her hair dry and like a wild frenzy of ferns framing her figure. By the time he left the boat with her wrapped in the blanket and cradled in his arms, still sleeping, it was dark and the lamplights of the pier cast shadows on the murky water. A dense fog had rolled in while he dealt with his catch and scrubbed the deck, and he walked her away from the water, laying her down in the cab of his truck and driving her down the winding back roads toward his small cabin tucked into the dark woods.

He slept like a child that night, the best night's sleep he had since he was a young boy, all the past mistakes that hounded him evaporated with her in the bed next to him. But when he woke at dusk, she was no longer beside him and he heard rustling and rummaging throughout the cabin, then a cry that sounded otherworldly shook through the house. In no rush, he pulled the blankets from his body and slipped on his slippers, lighting another smoke before leaving the bedroom. Resting his shoulder on the door frame, he watched her pace the house, pushing furniture violently, lifting the lids of baskets and boxes, each time eliciting the same mournful sound.

He took a drag before speaking, knowing exactly what she searched for, "You won't find it here."

Her eyes leapt up to meet him, the cool black liquid shimmered in the light and her face seemed feral and anguished.

"I've read about women like you. Heard fishermen tell stories. But you never believe them, not really, even if you always want to."

She sank to her knees, saltwater tears streaming down her cheeks.

"I've been alone a long time, Maria. Is it okay if I call you Maria?" he carried on without waiting for an acknowledgement; he knew there would be none. "I loved a girl once when I was younger, but I drove her away. I can be a bit controlling, you see. A bit possessive."

He crossed to her, lifted her chin to the air with a knuckle and pushed her wild hair behind her ear.

"But you won't leave me, will you Maria? Not without your second skin, which you won't find here."

The fire in her eyes seemed to dim right before his eyes, it cooled, like two black holes, empty and devoid of fight.

"There's a girl," he said, bending down and kissing her forehead, the faint scent of silt reaching his nose.

***

Years had passed with Maria in the cabin, gutting fish and roasting them over the fire, though she never got used to the taste of cooked fish. She spoke to no one this whole time, least of all her husband, saw no one. John kept her from the river, never once again bringing her to the boat. He never took her out of a short radius from the cabin. Sometimes he liked to take her into the woods, especially at night, and fuck her up against trees, down in the soil, on the mossy surfaces of the bodies of logs.

She learned how to vacate her body, imagining herself floating down the river. It didn't matter to the fisherman one bit whether she was in her body or out of it, as long as the body belonged to him. She became a husk of herself, which was ironic considering her actual husk, the shell that should be holding her, was kept somewhere else entirely. For the first year she spent every day he was away from the cabin fishing searching for her skin. Maria knew little of men before the day she had jumped on his boat but had been fascinated by the way they moved and their booming laughs. She had watched John for some time, so when the day finally came—her chance to shed her skin for a few hours and be with one, she took it. Not all selkies do, having a deep untrust for humans, but she was relatively young when she boarded his boat. She hadn't yet witnessed the cruelty of men, didn't understand that the rivers and oceans were filled with their garbage that trapped and mutilated and poisoned all the creatures she'd so desperately loved in the deep waters.

It had only been five years, but her hair had turned a shock of grey, like storm clouds all around her, the stress of being out of body for too long. She was wandering through the woods one day, a basket in hand, collecting mushrooms and berries, when she heard rustling ahead of her in the trees. She froze where she was, her bare feet cold in the damp soil. Though she had taken to covering up, wearing long shirts from her husband's dresser drawer, the damp and wetness of the coast never chilled her, and she had never taken to wearing shoes. As she stood still the rustling grew louder, closer, until a large black bear ambled out from the bushes before her. He sniffed the air, looking up to meet her gaze. They stood there for what felt like hours but could have only been minutes. The bear walked toward her, and she stayed still, having a keen animal sense that he meant her no harm. He sniffed the ground at her feet, up her legs, pushed on her stomach with his damp nose. She giggled, a noise she had never heard come from her body before, and the bear met her eyes, a growl much like a chortle escaping his lips. Reaching out, Maria stroked the bear's fur and he closed his eyes, leaning his head into her hands.

That is how it began. For months she met the black bear in the woods the minute John left for the boat. He must have sensed that something was different with Maria, for the hours when he was home became more tempestuous and volatile. He hurt her in ways he never had before, unable to pinpoint why he no longer trusted her, but knowing that something was intrinsically different. He grasped to control what he believed was rightfully his, but the minute he was gone she fled out the door. The bruises on her skin all shades of purple, black, blue, greens, and yellows. Her and the bear would wander through the woods, her collecting berries and him eating them right off the bushes. They took naps in the sun, her body nestled into the warmth of his fur and his giant claws cradling her head.

The bear, unable to keep away from her for long, began creeping ever nearer the cabin each night. He heard the cries of Maria one night, the full moon casting light through the dark windows, and he watched as John tossed her to the ground. A roar ripped through the atmosphere, shuddering the trees and the walls, sending bats spinning up into the sky. John ran outside, shotgun in hand, still in his house slippers, and the black bear charged him from the side of the house, knocking the gun to the ground, a shot ringing out into the empty abyss of trees. He attacked the man with such a frenzy, it wasn't until John lay dead on the ground, deep gouges covering his body, that the bear shifted. In the silence Maria came to the door and found the bear, crouched down and staring at the brown skin of his fingers where claws should be. Turning his hands over, he marveled how slender and delicate these new fingers were, how strange they seemed attached to his own body yet devoid of fur. He was soaked in the blood of the fishermen, and she went to him, lifting and bringing him inside. His body moved with a light agility he could never remember experiencing and when she put him under the shower and turned the water on, the heat on bare skin surprised him and he jumped back. She touched his back gently, guiding him back in, until he relaxed under the pressure of the manmade rain.

While he stood under the stream, she went back outside, dragged her husband's body to the fire barrel, the strength of her selkie body still intact. She started a fire then lifted his lifeless weight into the barrel. Back at the door, she found the black pelt the bear had shed and gathered it to her, pressing her face to its warmth before bringing it inside, laying it across the wooden table. Following the scent of moss to the bathroom, she pulled the bloody t-shirt off her head and stepped under the stream of water, joining the bear where he stood with his eyes closed under the steaming stream, moonlight trickling in through the open window, the smell of salt in the air.

Instinct

The dogs noticed the squirrel first. They were posted at the fence, barking wildly, racing up and down the side, as if the squirrel would pop up at any moment and they could assume chase. All day long they kept vigil. When they were released in the morning they ran straight to the fence and I followed them. There was the squirrel, in a different position than the day before. I crouched down to look at it, and its eye stared back at me. A dog barked and it started pushing itself across the dirt, trying to escape.

"It's okay. It's okay. It's okay," I said, and it settled down, breathing heavily, staring up at me.

I noticed the older neighbor out in his yard. "You've got a paralyzed squirrel over here in the sunflower garden. I thought it was dead yesterday, but it seems to be alive, just can't push itself."

I imagined crouching down and picking up the small creature delicately. You could tell it wasn't even a year old. Its body too small and slender—it hadn't yet hibernated, lived through a winter, grown fat on its food store.

I showed the man where it was while repeating, "It's okay. I'm sorry. It's okay. I'm sorry," to its eye that followed my movements. I got the loudest of my dogs corralled back into the house.

I shut the door and turned to see the man raise his shovel and come down on the little animal repeatedly.

"Thwack, thwack, thwack," I heard as I turned my body away.

Eventually the noise stopped as he buried the small fragile body in the ground of his garden, but the noise hasn't stopped in my head. All day and all night I hear it. I see the unblinking eye of trust staring up at me.

I haven't slept in three days. During the day I sit outside in the backyard with a book in hand but unopened. There are no squirrels chasing each other from tree to tree. My world is a ghost town.

The silence feels like a rupture. It is too peaceful.

I pick up my shovel.

The Girl with Dragonfly Wings
—*For Jordana*—

Josephine couldn't remember the last time she had flown. What used to come so natural had grown so far removed that she wasn't even sure what flight tasted like any more. She had some slight memory—when the wind caught her blue hair just right, whipped it up around her, that feeling of sailing through nothingness. The wild abundance of air around her gave her a strange tingling feeling right in the places where shoulder blades end and before spine begins. At night she closed her eyes and rested her head on a clump of moss she had gathered and plumped into a pillow. She slept in the back of the cave she found near the waterfall. An old tree that had grown out and over it, dripping moss from its branches to create a natural curtain. Josephine didn't have words for things such as pillow, or curtain, but she understood the minute she had taken human form and found herself with bare skin and long blue hair that matched the color of what used to be her body, that she required lots of sleep, and it was painfully uncomfortable to rest one's head on the hard earth. It was equally uncomfortable to feel exposed; as if her dragonfly body had been anything but.

At night she listened to the water crash into the rocks below it, and the crystal clear river trickled by, a mere 3 feet from the cave's entrance. There were things she knew or understood but didn't understand how she knew them or had acquired the information. She was sure it was somehow a product of the new large body she found herself in. For instance, she knew that when other humans came to the waterfalls to swim in the dark lagoon, that she must keep herself hidden. She crawled up over the edge of the falls, hidden behind ferns and rocks that were triple her size, and watched the humans splash around, touch one another in such a delicate way that it reminded her of what it felt like to have the wind caress her body. She shivered all over, up at the top in her hiding spot where she had to stay late one night when a pair of humans found their way to a large tree trunk that had fallen many storms ago, and in the dark of night intertwined their bodies in a way that made Josephine feel chilled to the bone. As she watched them move and bend their bodies in the same way the water curved and slid it's way around the river rocks she found it hard to breathe.

Josephine remembered the night she had transformed. There was a structure in the woods that she had been flying around all day. Zooming back and forth, weaving in and out and around. There was an old woman, hair long and silver like a kiss from a dragonfly's wings. Josephine had been attracted to the color of her hair, that much she could remember. The old woman had been bent over a patch of heirloom tomatoes, their aroma seeping up into the air, making indiscernible patterns on the sky. She had flown low, attracted to the silvery wisps of the old woman's hair that floated behind her as if they were full of static and a wild frantic buzzing that only Josephine could hear.

Right before Josephine had landed the old woman turned toward her as if she knew she were coming. She lifted her hand in perfect synchronicity, and Josephine landed on the tip of her pointer finger. She knew better than to get too near humans. She had been watching them for the whole 6 months of her life, and she found them to be clumsy at best, and downright cruel at their worst. But for some reason she wasn't afraid of the older woman whose hand she perched on, fluttering her wings, a perfect movement. Josephine knew that her time was ending, not in the way that humans measure time, but in the way that Nymphaea Red Flare water lily knows to open its delicate red petals and show off its dark-hearted center only in the evenings. The old woman with the shimmering hair knew her time was ending as well; she felt it in the unsteady thump that her heart now made, in the way that her eyes no longer wanted to open in the mornings, in the labored breath she had while doing nothing more than sipping her buttercream coffee. Her life had been a series of hazardous mistakes and misfortunes, bad choices and even worse men. She thought that if she could just make one right choice, one last ditch effort at redemption, to choose the way she left this world, to transform herself, if only for a day, then maybe it would make up for all the lost years and loneliness she had felt. The old woman lifted the bright blue dragonfly to eye-level.

"Are you here to take me home?" she asked

Josephine lifted her wings to the air, flew up and landed delicately on the parched and cracked lips of the woman whose name she'd never know. The old woman crumpled at the dragonflies touch. Her clothes melted down around her, her body disappeared, and up from the pale yellow sundress that lay on the ground flew the most pristine silver dragonfly that Josephine had ever seen. It flew off in the direction of the sunset, and Josephine was too stunned to fly after it.

Eventually she turned and cut a direct path to the waterfall she often flew over, just high enough to not have her wings damaged by the thrash and crash of the water. She landed on the edge of the river, the cream colored moon above; the next thing she knew, her body was a long and sinewy thing, her skin creamy like a liquid moon. Just as she had released the old woman from the shell of herself, she too had been granted something. Time. She felt time in the lean muscles in her thighs and rounded bottom when she pushed herself off the ground.

She felt the time in the way her arms and legs pumped when she walked into the river, bathed herself in the cool reflected surface of the dark pool under the waterfall. Josephine felt the possibility of time the night she watched the couple bend, release, break, and come back together on the trunk of the 100 year old tree. She felt where her wings had been, a deep hollow ache she was sure she would always feel. But she also felt something else, the flutter from her wings had been shifted, she felt it in the pit of her stomach, in the wells of her chest.

One day soon, she would walk out from the cave where she slept. It would happen on a cloud covered day, when the world around her was full of misty air and a fog so thick that she couldn't see anything in front of her except the man standing alone at the water's edge. When he would turn to see her, he would blink repeatedly, unable to believe that what his clear blue eyes were seeing wasn't a figment of his imagination, a dream come to life. Her deep blue hair would fall around her shoulders and she'd walk across the river rocks as if they were a lush bed of carpet and not in fact, stone. Afterwards, she would finally come to understand what it meant to be human, what it felt like when the wrong man loves a woman, how the touch of a hand on her back—placed at the exact spot where the shoulder blades end and before the spine begins—can feel like the way that wings beat in the darkest part of the night. Josephine would learn what it feels like to be a woman with a cavern inside her heart and an emptiness that overflows. She'd learn what it felt to be a woman with invisible dragonfly wings beating underneath her breast.

Here is where I loved you

"Outside I can see my past. Here is where I stood with a friend and talked about a movie. Here is the exact moment I knew I wanted to write. Here's the bed I slept in with someone I once loved. Here is the weather when I had bronchitis. Here is the emotion when I said goodbye."   —Amina Cain, *Creature*

I am driving down winding backroads, one boy in the passenger's seat, three in the back, one of whom is my boyfriend, and on his lap sits my best friend, her long hair whipping out the back-driver's side window so I can see it in my side mirror. We are at the end of adolescence here. It is late summer and sunshine is blazing through the open windows while Tech N9ne blasts from the stereo. We are in our bathing suits and on our way to the Alderbrook Pier to go swimming.

In the back of the dodge neon are bottles of seven-dollar rum. Every one of us is smoking Marlboro Reds. I am driving the car but then I am looking in the rear-view mirror. And even though I am still driving the car I am no longer driving it. I'm not even a passenger anymore, the only thing attaching me to the seat is the cigarette, slowly burning out the window in my hand. In the back seat, as if from a great distance, I see my boyfriend, already drunk, lean in to my best friends' hair. Without thinking, he kisses her on the side of the forehead and her large blue doe-eyes bulge. She turns toward the mirror and sees me in it, looking back at her. My whole body, so familiar with these roads, careens the car to safety while my eyes stay on hers. I can see, before we park, that his hands are resting up on top of the bare skin of her thighs. We pull up to the tall grasses and the bright yellow scotch broom, invasive, overtaking the marshy meadow.

Everyone is in jovial spirits and I pretend to be, though I am separate from them all and I can feel my separateness like an extra limb—like a bug on my skin crawling, but when I look down to swat it nothing is there. I take one of the bottles of rum and began housing it, though I am the only one here with a license and a car. I will be the one to drive us home later. I have never driven drunk, though I've driven high on weed or pills plenty of times.

We head on to the trail and in the bright yellow petals of scotch broom are large webs or cocoons, I'm not sure which, but they stare back at me all the same. We are both in knots. We walk through a section of tall grass and I remember the video on my old flip phone that my boyfriend and I took of ourselves, naked and all body parts. His pale legs between my summer tanned thighs. Someone lights a blunt and we pass it up and down the trail until we reach the Columbia River which sits dark teal blue before us, water lapping inwards. We drink until the tide begins to go out, pulling us with it on the draft of the booze.

I am standing with my friend some feet down the pier from the boys. We haven't said a word about what I saw and what she knows that I saw. We won't ever. Something inside me is broken, but the alcohol is masking it and I want to see what he sees in her, my best friend who I now know is sleeping with my boyfriend behind my back. I imagine them sitting together in her room, where I sit with her. Doing lines of pills off her light wood stool where I do lines with her, and then falling into bed afterwards. I am thinking of all the times I've come over after getting off an 8-hour shift while neither of them has jobs. I enter the apartment and her mom says hi if she isn't already nodded out in her recliner as I walk by the living room without knocking at the door first. They are always sitting in her bedroom with the door open, a few feet apart, waiting for me to arrive.

I lean in, drunk, and kiss her on the lips. I feel the pressure of her lips on my lips and find that her lips are soft and singular. I want to know more about this singularity. One of the boys notices what we are doing and we pull from each other, clasp hands, and laughing, run and jump off the pier. Our hands still clasped all the way down until our feet sink into the silt of the river and I want to stay down there. It isn't that I consciously think this. It is that I hold her hand and don't let go until she pulls from me and then I remember to push off the ground and shoot back up into the lap of the ice-cold waves on my body. We are laughing again when we are above water. We are desperately fighting off the tide of what has been lost today.

We are in the car again, just me and my best friend. The sun is setting and the boys are waiting for us to get back from a cigarette run. Somehow, I must have driven us back safely to her apartment, but now on the couple block drive to the Shell station I laugh at something she says, turning to look at her face as I do so, and I hit the curb full on right before we park.

Outside of the car we look down at the flattened tire. We are still in our bathing suits and the warm summer breeze feels good. Everything feels funny, even this, a drunk driving accident with my tire as the only casualty. Her cousin, one of the boys we'd been with all day, runs down from the apartment when we call him and changes my tire. He is laughing too, we are all laughing even though nothing is funny, but his face looks like a burst of sunlight and when I imagine him, all these years now passed since he overdosed in the woods, I still see the way his thick eyebrows, almost a unibrow but not quite, crinkled in the middle of his forehead with his smile.

Later, still trying to blind my eyes from what I had seen, I take a pill. When I blearily awake, it is pitch black outside and I am on her bedroom couch alone. I stumble to the open window and throw up all down the side of the apartment from the second floor. Then, I walk to her extended closet where her bed is pushed back into the space and find her and my boyfriend asleep, bodies separate, but they are in their underwear. I feel both inside my body and outside of it. I reach in and wake them up. I remember nothing after that, as if my heartbreak eclipsed the entire night. No moon left in my sky. In the morning, everyone acts like nothing happened. We keep playing pretend, for a little while longer. Months later, I sit on her couch while I text his best friend. I leave him for his friend and when I do, I leave her. I blow it all up. I am a torpedo. I am all cannon and fire and battle axe. I break everything around me.

When I get sober I look at everything around me. I am farther away than ever before, but somehow, I am still driving that car. They are in the backseat. Even though she's dead now too, in my backseat, her blonde hair is blowing out the window.

On the Alderbrook pier, her hand is in my hand as we leap off the edge, feet first into the tide. On the side of the road, our dried-out bathing suits smell like river mud and I turn to her, laughing.

Bureau of Evaporation

Fiona remained, to her knowledge, the only person who could see the process of evaporation. When she was five, she witnessed her first evaporation, though really the disappearance of her father began when she was around three. It began with a slow fading; small pieces of him went missing: a fingernail, a chunk of hair, the tip of his nose. Eventually larger chunks of him disappeared. One day her dad would be strumming on his acoustic guitar, the next he would be missing a finger from his dominant hand, then two, then three. He would go into the bathroom with two ears and come out with only one. One day he bent to catch Fiona as she slid down a slide at the park and when he stood up a kneecap had vanished.

Her father's disappearance was gradual.

Fiona lay on her belly on the rug drawing while her dad took a nap in the rocking chair next to the fireplace. By this time nearly all her dad was missing except for his wide-set and serious mouth and his green eyes that at one point had been sparkly and energetic but had grown duller and darker over time. As a young child, she didn't understand what was happening and even if she had, she wouldn't have had the language to explain it. She could still hear his voice when he read her a bedtime story. She could feel his hand as he swept her pale curls out of her eyes even though his hands had been one of the first things to fully go. And she could always see where he was because his clothing didn't disappear with him.

On the day of evaporation her mom left to run errands. While her dad napped, Fiona pretended there was a maiden with wild, long blonde hair riding the back of the black stallion she held in her hand. The maiden's hair was thick with ivy, moss, and twigs, and she was on a mission to save a prince from a tower where he had been trapped, unseen by all those who passed nearby for his whole life. Just as the maiden and stallion reached the castle tower, her dad let out a long sigh, shaking Fiona from her daydream. She glanced up at him just in time to see the last pieces of her dad disappear altogether. His eyelids popped open in surprise, as if he could feel his mouth disappearing. Their eyes locked one last time before he vanished entirely. There was a whoosh of air; a snap echoed through the room followed by a sizzle as her dad's clothes crumpled to the floor at the place where his invisible feet had been touching the ground.

Fiona gathered his clothes in her hand, trying to grasp his invisible limbs that were no longer there. Upon returning home, Fiona's mom, Marian, tried to ask Fiona where her dad went, but she only wept into his plaid shirt gripped inside her small hands. Marian searched the house for her missing husband, and when she couldn't find him, she searched for signs he had left her and their young daughter, but his suitcase was still stored in the top of the closet. His wallet and keys lay on the bedside table and all his socks and underwear were still tucked safely inside the dresser drawers.

Panicked, Marian finally dialed the police. She had heard of the disappearances. Everyone had, though it was a secret they hid from Fiona, as she was too young to have her imagination and laughter tempered by the harsh terrors of the world. On more than one occasion they had discussed how Fiona must have overheard something about the disappearances from somewhere and using her childlike sense of *other* had made sense of the disappearances in the only way she knew how, by imagining her father as slowly disappearing.

When the two detectives showed up at her door Marian explained every moment since she had gotten home, but when the three adults tried again to question Fiona she sat still, staring blankly into the empty rocking chair, still clutching her dad's favorite shirt.

"Disappeared.   Disappeared.   Disappeared," she whispered to herself.

The adults gave up and stepped away from her and the female detective with the kind eyes leaned towards Marian, "I am sorry to say this, but the likelihood of your husband being found is almost non-existent."

Fiona let out a wail that echoed the sounds of the sirens as they had sounded minutes before when they pulled up outside of their house.

For months after her father's evaporation Fiona watched her mom carefully, waiting for the moment when she too would begin to disappear. Marian's eyes were sunken in, she had bags underneath them, and her rosy complexion had faded to a gray hue. There was no ceremony held for disappearances, no memorial service, no way to properly mourn something that was unknowable. Fiona was sure that any minute her mother's skin would begin to fade, but it never did. When Marian thought that Fiona wasn't looking at her she would sometimes get lost standing by the window looking out at the world or staring into the eyes of her husband in an old picture frame. In these moments Fiona would catch it, the electricity in the air, and her mom would flicker like a lightbulb that is thinking about dying, but then Marian would look down at Fiona and her form would become more solid than it had been before. She was still lonely and grieving, but solid nonetheless. Her mom's desire to exist for her daughter seemed to overcome the mere idea of disappearance.

By the time Fiona was born people had been disappearing for around seven years. At first people thought nothing of it. Those who leave or go missing oftentimes turn back up in another state, or they come back home, or sometimes their bodies are found in unlikely places. It took a few months for anyone to notice that these disappearances were different. Those who went missing seemed to utterly vanish, one minute there, the next gone, with no sign of having taken anything with them, not even the clothes that had been on their backs. The world is littered with debris, so piles of random clothes didn't immediately trigger any alarm bells. And although a few people claimed to have seen a person disappear right before their eyes, they were brushed off as crazy or letting their imaginations get away with them. Especially as those who disappeared were often the type of people who felt alone, those ignored, rejected, and forgotten.

Once the world began to take notice, there was little to be done, since one hundred percent of those that disappeared remained unfound. Religious zealots claimed it was the rapture, finally and at last, but they did admit that the rapture happened slower than they ever imagined it would. One by one the people went missing. One by one the religious fell to their knees in prayer, whispers echoing, *take me.* Of course, there were plenty of other theories: alien abductions, government sanctions, the illuminati. None of these did anything to help those who were left behind. Nor did any of these theories help to find the disappeared. The scientists tested the remaining clothes, took air particle samples from the homes or places where the person in question was last seen, but they found nothing. There was simply a complete absence of evidence to point in any one direction.

***

The disappearances were most alarming when they happened to a child. There are few things more disturbing than a missing child. About the only thing worse than a child missing is a child dead, but with what the world knew of evaporations, they might as well have been. The year after her father's evaporation two children in Fiona's school disappeared. The first was a fourth grader and as such Fiona never had a chance to see him or recognize the signs of evaporation. Fourth and fifth graders took lunch at a different time and had an entirely different playground, and it just so happened that this boy, Bobby Redmond, lived on the opposite side of town, so they took entirely different bus routes. In fact, it was on this bus that Bobby's clothes had been discovered with the boy no longer inside them. He had climbed on the bus on an early foggy morning at the end of his rundown street and sat in the very backseat where he always sat alone.

Rumor had it that Bobby was a lonesome boy; he took up very little space and easily went unnoticed. On more than one occasion other children had nearly sat down on him before noticing he was there. Bobby wasn't the first child to have gone missing from Livingston Heights, but they didn't usually disappear while at school or en route; usually their evaporation took place at home or somewhere in the outdoors: at a park where all that was left were shorts crumpled on the ground and a t-shirt dangling off a swing, in the woods behind the child's house, or sometimes even in an aisle smackdab in the middle of a grocery store.

The second child to go missing that year was a girl from Fiona's first grade class. Her name was Rachel Petrovsky, and she had long brown curls. She too mostly kept to herself. Fiona began noticing Rachel fading. At first it just seemed that her color was dimming but then one day Rachel wore a long brown skirt to class and when she reached above her head to grab her jacket out of the cubby hole for recess Fiona spotted it. At the bottom of her right leg where there should have been an ankle there was none. There was a thin and bony calf and a bright red leather shoe, but no ankle holding the two together. Up until the fourth grader had disappeared and news of it spread throughout the school, Fiona was unaware that children could evaporate too. With this new knowledge she found herself more on edge than ever. She'd been keeping a watchful eye on the other students, becoming friendlier with them to spot the warning signs. She had tried, on previous occasions, to break through Rachel Petrovsky's brick like exterior to no avail.

Rachel's parents were immigrants, and though she had been born in this land, she had a hint of a Russian accent when she spoke. The kids weren't necessarily cruel about her accent, but each could feel her difference and in kindergarten she had been separate from the masses, feeling that deep inside she was somehow irrevocably as different as the others believed her to be.

With Rachel's increasing invisibility Fiona continued to try and engage the girl in conversation over the next few months, but the girl just stared at her blankly behind the sheath of her hair. Parts of Rachel seemed to disappear at a much faster rate than that of Fiona's dad. Fiona thought that maybe it was because her father was much larger compared to Rachel's size. He had more of his body to hold on to. Fiona started keeping a journal, tracking the goings of Rachel's body parts, as well as any interactions or lack of interactions she witnessed regarding her. Once she started keeping record, she noticed something startling. Rachel never talked to anyone. Ever. Mrs. Earnest never called on her in class, nor pulled her aside to have a word with her. It was a large class of nearly 30 students around or under the age of 6, and Fiona noted how busy Mrs. Earnest always seemed to be, too busy to have much concern over the disappearing girl who shrank down her body in the back row of the class.

It was May, and the school year was coming to an end. The other students were exuberant in their excitement for the freedom of summer, and the fresh smell of flowers and cut grass turned them into wild animals. All but two students rampaged around like wild boars, pulling each other's hair, playing tag at recess until they fell into the grass, breath coming in gasps while they tried to catch it. Two girls were not among them. The first girl sat at a picnic table, forever scribbling away in her journal. The second girl, only noticed by the first girl, made a cave for herself under the lip of the giant slide. All that could be seen of the second girl by the first girl was her brown curls flying in the wind and a paisley pink dress lying down in the grass.

Fiona felt a charge in the air. She slammed her journal shut and began to run to where Rachel lay. She was no more than five feet away when Rachel's dark hair flickered and flashed. She heard it, the *snap*; the *sizzle*. Rachel's dress crumpled to the ground. No one else noticed. No one else saw. Where there used to be a girl who thought herself too strange to be loved laid an empty dress and two red shoes. Fiona ran to get Mrs. Earnest who was in the process of pulling two wild boys off each other.

"She's gone," Fiona gasped as she tugged on Mrs. Earnest's jacket sleeve.

"Who's gone, dear?"

"Rachel. Rachel Petrovsky. She was laying under the slide, and now she is gone. Just like my dad," Fiona began to cry.

Mrs. Earnest bristled. She tried to conjure a picture of Rachel in her mind but found that she only had the faint impression of a small child with brown curls and red shoes.

"Bring me to her," she said, no longer locked in a battle with the two boys who had straightened up at Fiona's cries. In fact, all the playground was still and silent as Fiona led their teacher by the hand to the large metal slide where Rachel's dress lay.

Fiona pointed, now afraid to go too near.

"Oh, dear," one of Mrs. Earnest's hands flew to cover her mouth as she bent down to pick up one of the two red leather shoes that lay in a pile at the bottom of the paisley print dress.

A small boy who stood near the slide but had not noticed the girl that had laid underneath, saw the red shoes and with enthusiasm said, "Maybe she tapped her shoes together and shouted, 'Home! Home! Home!'"

A couple of the other children laughed nervously.

Mrs. Earnest turned to the boy, "Charlie, run and get the principal."

Charlie blinked back at her, startled out of his reverie of fairy tales and magic red shoes.

"Go," Mrs. Earnest urged before kneeling next to the clothes, as if holding a vigil for the girl's return.

***

After the evaporation of Rachel Petrovsky, Fiona began keeping detailed records of anyone that she was suspicious of disappearing or that showed what she referred to as 'markers' for possible evaporation. These markers included people who hardly ever spoke, who kept to the back of rooms, who hunched their shoulders or made themselves small, but it also grew to mean people who were uncared for: the homeless man who lived on the edge of the park, the brazen young woman who made herself like steel as protection because too many times had she been left unprotected and alone, the melancholy old man who sat on the edge of a duck pond every day, hands buried in his pockets, a grimace on his face.

No detail was too small for her records. If she saw a person who was missing pieces of themselves she recorded the date and time, what the person was wearing, where she saw them, what pieces of them were missing, and she drew detailed maps of the person's location. This was especially useful when taking notice of people she didn't know. A lady with thick black braids who worked the checkout line at the local grocery was missing her right cheekbone and her left elbow. A man in a yellow car at the stop light next to them had only half a face and when he picked his nose he seemed to be digging around in invisible air. The old man with the tangled grey beard, who looked like he may have been a sailor at one point, and who stood at the corner of Division and Franklin holding a cardboard sign that said, "Bet you can't hit me with a quarter," was missing his entire left arm, half of his mouth, and his right eye. It seemed that each time Fiona and her mom drove by that intersection more of the man went missing until one day where the man had stood was a pile of beaten and battered clothes, two mismatched boots, and a cardboard sign with the letters in sharpie looking up at the sky.

It wasn't only disappearing people that Fiona took note of in her records. She also had a detailed list and map of anywhere she saw piles of clothes. The intersection of Franklin and Division where the man without a home evaporated was a hotspot for missing people. Nearby there was what the city called 'a homeless camp' and anywhere within a fifty foot radius of that area—and all down the side streets surrounding it—piles of clothes could be found. Though the government was aware of the disappearances and that what a person was wearing at the time of disappearance was always left behind, they seemed to do little in the way of cleaning up the remnants of a human existence.

By the time Fiona was sixteen years old she had filled over 27 journals with notes on evaporations, and the piles of clothes that littered the world grew exponentially. The world seemed to have given up any hope of solving the mystery. It was as if there was an unspoken agreement between people that extended far beyond sexes, races, and class systems. Or maybe it was a fear similar to that of a curse—that if they spoke of the act of disappearing, they would be the next to go. The religious zealots gave up their pursuit of being taken in rapture. They went one of two ways: they either lost all belief in their God, or they surmised that they weren't worthy and as such had been left behind, either way it made them feel abandoned and reckless, and this reckless abandonment often led to a slow deterioration until they got what they thought they wanted, and all that was left was a Sunday dress or a pile of shiny shoes and khaki pants.

Over the years her mom had given up on trying to see inside the journals that her daughter always had at least one of on her person. Fiona kept the journals in a padlock box under her bed, one only she knew the code to. Marian, happy to still have her daughter, never married again, but eventually her flickers grew less and less. Fiona became sure that her mother would in fact live to whatever natural age she was meant for and would be taken from this earth in a manner that was fitting and normal, whatever way that would be. Having the gift to see evaporation in process had isolated Fiona, but not in a way that harmed her as a person, because it gave her a purpose. And as she learned from years of observing and cataloging evaporations, purpose could make all the difference. She never felt as if she was lacking from it, and inside school she did her work diligently. She had a symbiotic-working relationship with her peers and her teachers. They didn't outright avoid her, they just didn't interact with her outside of the school setting, but this was fine. Fiona was busy balancing schoolwork and her meticulous records.

Today, as she walked home from school on a trail that took her around the edge of Parkland Park, a name which she always thought lacked a certain amount of creativity, she noted a blue plaid shirt, a pair of jeans with a hole in one knee, and a dirty white pair of Reebok tennis shoes on the other side of the fence. Nearby someone had cut a hole in the fencing with wire-cutters. Clearly this person had been making a home for themselves outside when they disappeared, as a blue tarp lay a few feet away, having been blown in the wind overnight. Fiona crossed the park and sat down on the end of a slide where she could view the clothes and the fence.

Not only did she take notes, but she had become quite the artist. Her notebooks were filled with dates, times, locations, and images of empty clothes in heaps and bundles at the end of a street, on a bathroom floor at a shopping center, at the top of the stairs that led to the train, behind a tree trunk on the trails that led to Mt. Leo. The pictures, drawn with pencil and shaded in immaculately, had a quality of sorrow to them that was hard to articulate. Fiona's art professor, Ms. Francis, had caught a glimpse of them when she passed behind Fiona shading one in on the bleachers at lunch. The power that emanated from the work slammed into her chest and she froze, nearly tipping her cafeteria slice of pizza on top of Fiona's head. When she asked to see more of her work, Fiona tentatively showed her a few of the drawings: a pile of rain-soaked clothes built up below a freeway underpass, a rain jacket, a black dress, and bright yellow rain boots with flamingos printed on the sides lay serenely on the ground at the base of a bench in the park, a woman's one-piece mint green swimsuit floated openly on the top of Lake Baxter.

"Oh. My," Ms. Francis whispered, pulling the notebook closer to her purple rimmed glasses. "These are...miraculous."

Fiona had never thought of them as anything other than a snapshot of evidence, like a photo taken at the scene of a crime. Her cheeks colored, "Uh, thanks."

Ms. Francis began to flip frantically through the notebook from one image to another, ignoring altogether the pages filled with words and spreadsheets and maps, enraptured by the piles of missing clothes, reminding her so much of the two piles of clothes she found ten years ago at the ground of the porch swing of her elderly parent's house that she now lived in.

"Have you thought of entering any of these in an exhibit Fiona? I think they would do well." She didn't wait for Fiona's reply before adding, "There is a school exhibit coming up in April." She handed the journal back, "You should submit. I am going to put your name down on the list. The art room is filled with empty canvases, feel free to come by and take some home with you."

Before Fiona could reply Ms. Francis made her way down to the other end of the bleachers where a small group of teachers clustered together on the uncommonly warm January day. Fiona flipped through the images she had drawn, seeing them in a new way. She'd never thought of them as art. She was too busy recording the next sighting, a silent partner of evaporation, but now she saw a glimmer of something outside of the electric air and volatile snap that she dreamed about every night. Later that week she stuck her head around the corner of the art room door to see if anyone was inside.

Ms. Francis looked up from her desk, "Ah, yes! Fiona! I am so happy to see you. I've been waiting for you." She walked over to the blank canvas storage unit. "What size were you thinking?"

"Umm," Fiona drew out in a long breath, "I'm not really sure."

"How about I give you two 5 by 7 canvases and one 7 by 10? Three seems like a good number. The bigger one can be the center of the other two on display?" Ms. Francis asked as she gathered the blank canvas's and crossed the room where she picked out three charcoal pencils from her own personal desk. "These should do nicely," she handed the pencils and canvases to Fiona before pushing her frazzled red hair off her face, wiping a line of charcoal on her forehead which had transferred from her hand to her head.

"Uh, sure." Fiona said, mostly unsure, but with a strange sensation blooming in her chest she smiled at Ms. Francis as she took the supplies, "Sure. Yes."

Ms. Francis clapped her hands together, "Wonderful!"

Fiona looked down at the canvas and pencils in her hands and back up at the teacher, "What if they don't turn out like the drawings in the notebook? I've never worked on canvas before or with charcoal."

"You can't know until you fill in the invisible spaces." She put a hand on Fiona's shoulder, "There is no harm in trying."

Fiona placed the pencils in her backpack and held the canvases tight to her chest. Her long pale hair swept around her face and across the empty white spaces of the boards she held against her body. As she turned to leave Ms. Francis called out to her while she passed through the open door.

"Fiona. It is okay to want something for yourself."

Fiona tilted her head to the side, pondering something.

"Everybody, even the loneliest of us, especially the loneliest, want to be seen. I think your drawings can do that for someone. I think they can cast a light on those that feel unseen."

Fiona thought over this as she turned once again to go.

"Ms. Francis," Fiona paused and looked at her teacher once more, "Do you think noticing something, taking note, can stop someone from disappearing?"

"I think it is a start."

***

Everyone hovered around the black and white image of a little blond girl laying on her stomach in front of a fireplace, toy pony in hand, at the foot of an empty rocking chair. Next to the girl on the floor was a pile of empty clothes. If you looked hard or long enough at the rocking chair, the soft silhouette of an invisible man might take form. Fiona stood to the side, amazed at the reception of her center piece of work, the one drawn on the larger canvas. Staring at the silhouette she felt a rush of melancholy fold around her, but more than that, there was a sense of her father's presence in the air. If she closed her eyes, she was sure she'd smell sawdust and shaving cream. Capturing his evaporation, having others witness this, had brought her father into the room.

A boy from Fiona's history class came and stood near her. She had been keeping records of the boy's slow disappearance for months. His was one of the slowest evaporations she had yet to experience. It began with freckles, then the small mole that sat just below his dark brown hairline at the bottom of his neck. Next it was an invisible line that streaked across his cheek. Fiona had drawn him in her notebook one day, the only existing human ever to be drawn in her record of evaporations, when she saw him sitting on the bench in the park. She could faintly see the tree-line through the hollow space of his cheek. She turned to look at him now, never having spoken to him before.

"Hi, Fiona," he said, rubbing one arm with invisible hand.

"Oh. Hi Wyatt."

"I just wanted to say, I really like your work. It's like you captured it."

She raised an eyebrow, "Captured what?"

"What it feels like." He looked down at his invisible hand and held it up to the light, "To disappear."

Fiona's eyes widened.

Impulsively she reached out and grabbed his empty hand. The air felt electric. The hair on their arms raised. Wyatt's hand flickered, as if trying to take form. They both gasped in unison.

"Did you feel that?" Wyatt said.

And Fiona squeezed his hand.

Pomegranate Seeds & the Hearts of Men

If it wasn't for the cat she adopted from the Humane Society, she wouldn't have made it through the year. She named him Zeus, for he was haughty and full of himself, knowing full well he could demand affection and receive it, even if moments before he had rejected her advances. Zeus hopped off the couch as soon as she reached out her rogue red sharpened nails to pet his calico fur.

"You should respect the old gods," she said to him, to which he turned his ass in her direction, walking away with his tail lifted, as if to say, "Lady, I am the old gods."

The fan above clicked tirelessly in its rotation, coated in a layer of dust. The September wildfire light cast eerie orange silhouettes on the peeling walls and fake hardwood floors. She despised this apartment and everything it represented. Human's stacked one on top of the other, cage on a cage on a cage, and down in the soil below that, a burial ground lost to the peoples whose ancestors were buried there. The detritus of the building crumbling above them. The worst part is the humans rarely realized what they were: animals in a zoo that nobody longed to look at, to look after, to feed or care for.

Through the open window she could hear a neighbor watering the dying potted ferns sat in rows before her door. The sound of a shopping channel drifted down from somewhere, and she imagined perfectly the woman on the screen, hair locked in with too much hair spray, the scent practically wafting through the screen, and the look of utter derision, falsified as a smile, plastered across her pastel pink lipstick, the shade of loneliness and despair. The woman on the screen would be wearing fake pearls, a pastel button-up dress cinched at the waist to accentuate her breasts hoisted up in the grip of a nauseatingly tight bra, and the woman who watched the woman on the screen thought that maybe if she bought the product the tv woman held in her hands, her husband wouldn't breeze past her on his way in and out to work without a backwards glance. The woman would buy the product and nothing would change and a little bit more of her would die inside.

Lamia refused bras. She refused cosmetics—besides her blood-red nail polish—and all jewelry expect for the scarab beetle ring she wore on her middle finger. She didn't need excess, and in fact, abhorred it in others. The polish and ring weren't excess though, they were warning, one which so often wasn't heeded. The consumerism of today's people made her sick. She waited tables at the local dive to pay the exorbitant rent on this rundown apartment that sat near the woods at the edge of town. She could have made her money the old-fashioned way, as single women trying to get by in the world had in a million lifetimes before. As she had before. But in her old age she had grown tired of the type of men who paid for favors. Weak. Often filled with equal parts cowardice and contempt. The meat on their bones was rancid, sick with the scent of desperation, or worse, soft-hearted entitlement.

It wasn't that the men she took home from the diner weren't filled with this same putrid lust. They were often booze filled, homesick, heartsick, or worse by far, love struck. But at least she didn't have to pretend to enjoy them. If they were tiresome, she made quick work of them, then padded out, her bare feet clacking like talons on floors, placing a tin can up to the electric can opener, the whir of the blade slicing through the silence, filling the void where before had been screams.

A sharp wind rattled the used-to-be-white blinds in the window, and she calculated how many hours she had between now and her next shift. Grabbing the unopened pack of smokes off the coffee table, she tapped the top on her exposed upper thigh rhythmically before peeling off the seal. The cat came out of the bedroom and stared at her from the end of the hallway while licking his tender paws clean.

"Now who is the one willing to take my scraps, Zeus," she said, not to the cat.

She cranked her zippo across her skin and took a long drag in, the cigarette end crackling to life.

They used to say she went after men because of what was done to her, her children taken and left in their wake a lust for blood. That was just a rumor. The people always wanted reason, and what better reason than a woman being unmothered? The imagination of men was truly so small. As insignificant as the not yet children she had done away with herself, fluid filled sacs in the womb. They never grow out of it, those little boys. Generations and centuries of men and they still can't conceive of a woman whose soul purpose in life wasn't to burst forth more starving babies. More creatures to poison the seas, tear up the forests they needed in order to breathe. Their ignorance was laughable.

It wasn't what they did to her that made her ravenous. Really, they could do very little too her, though they never knew that when they climbed into the cab of her pickup. It was their utter complete lack of imagination that drove her to do it again and again. It had driven her all along. It wasn't madness but it was something close to. She only went after the ones who—even if they tried to keep their true feelings secret in today's modern world, their women standing next to them in their pink pussy hats—bit-by-bit, stole their women's freedoms through catfish troll accounts online and on the ballots and through quiet votes cast with their hands behind their backs, thumbs twiddling.

She had no female friends, no friends at all, other than the cat. She loved women, their sensuous hearts and lilting laughs. Staying separate was a matter of self-preservation. She could not be weakened by her needs. Lamia had loved a goddess before, but gods were like men, maybe even more so, possessive and unyielding. This is how she became what she is, after all, what she had long now been. For her love of Hera and all Hera loved, she had paid with a thousand lives, a thousand more. And for this price, for protecting the sacred hearts of women, she was allowed a secret that even Zeus the cat would never be allowed in on.

For it was in her slumber after sucking the bones dry that she fell into a deep sleep, a sleeping world where Hera waited for her, all silk and soul of her, draping around and through Lamia like a turbulent and soft wind.

It was Zeus who had done it, who had caught them and turned her into what she was. Unfortunately for him, he didn't get to decide who she turned her rage on, who she became the protector of. By day she devoured the hearts of men, and by night Hera fed her pomegranate seeds in her dreams.

Zeus the cat mewled quietly beside her, tilting his head inquisitively, and for a moment a blade of terror cut through her, imagining that this cat she named was linked to its namesake, transmitting her thoughts. She laughed at her own ridiculous paranoia and patted his head, not unkindly, before standing up from the couch. She slid her feet into red suede shoes and grabbed her keys and purse off the hook before unlatching the front door.

"Don't wait up," she winked at the cat and could have sworn he winked back.

She stepped outside into the smoky air. It filled her lungs. There was a thick layer of ash on her truck. She had seen more empires collapse than she could recall. It wouldn't be long left for this civilization, at least not in the years of gods and demons alike. This world was ripe for burning and she'd be there on the side, the cleanup crew, waiting for the next round of monsters and men.

Cranking the key a few times, she fired up the engine, lit another smoke, and drove to the heart of town where she would serve the people and then take out the trash.

Tower of Butterflies

She read about the butterfly migration in a novel and then spent hours looking at images and videos of butterflies amassing onto a field, then swirling around and up into the sky, majestic in their fluttering dance. It seemed her world was full of butterflies: the wings of the maple tree leaves that floated down beginning in early September, the red butterfly rash she sometimes got across the bridge of her nose, the thyroid gland in her throat that spread out in size as if the butterfly that was wedged there had stuffed itself with all her hopes and dreams and swallowed them alive.

When the white butterflies floated around her backyard, her dog, the only thing she had left from the divorce, would lunge around trying to catch them in his mouth. She would yell at him, do anything to distract him for a moment, long enough for the butterfly to make its escape. When she was a little girl, her mom had told her to never touch them. She claimed that touching a butterfly's wings would irreparably damage them because of the oils humans have on their hands, and to rob a butterfly of flight would only bring pain and suffering.

When the thyroid cancer came everyone was surprised, as if this was a disease that cared about age or time. There was nothing that could be done, the cancer had spread its wings and taken flight.

At 33 she purchased a ticket to fly and see the migration at the Sierra Madres in Mexico. She thought she would have more time. The whole flight she dreamed her arms had turned to perfectly matching speckled wings. When she arrived, she walked out into the field and stood stock still. One by one they began to land on her until she looked like nothing more than a tower of butterflies, and when the butterflies took flight all that was left was an empty void where she should have been.

Seeking Soul Mate at the Granada Theater

The Granada Theater opened its doors in 1948, and I have been haunting the place for almost as long. I always thought that ghosts would look like they did on the day they died, but it turns out *Beetlejuice* almost got it right. I float through the building in what is the equivalent of a white sheet with holes cut in the eyes. I can't remember what I used to look like. It's been far too long, but at the bottom of the sheet a pair of black and white oxford's poke out, so I imagine I must have been something to see, bold enough to pull off shoes like that. The theater is filled with mirrors and I spend a lot of time standing in front of them. Sometimes the girl with the violet hair notices me as I pass by, usually mistaking me for a customer, only to discover the lobby empty. I don't think she can truly see me when she is looking straight at me.

There is a stairway from the basement that they closed off, replaced the wall and doorway with a floor to ceiling mirror. I hear talk, apparently, this is where I died, but I don't really remember when or how or why. Language doesn't leave you when you die. My mind is a functioning machine, but who I was and how I died left me long ago. I sometimes stand at the top of the stairs and watch the customers. Small children often see me, see the stairwell behind the mirror, and run smack dab into the glass. This makes me chuckle a little, though I know it must hurt; when you're a ghost you also forget what pain feels like. If I want to pass through a wall or a mirror I do so without a second thought. The girl with the violet hair likes to keep the stairwell mirror very clean. I think she knows I'm in there. Sometimes she stands in front of the mirror staring in. I raise one of my sheeted hands and she does the same, a mirror image. I raise the other; again, she mimics my movements.

The manager of the theater doesn't believe in me. I can tell by the way his eyebrows raise whenever one of the employees claims that something spooky is afoot. *It's me*, I want to say, *It's my spooky feet*. I can't speak to any of them. Language may not be gone, but my ability to talk is. I try to communicate with them in other ways. I just want to be seen. At night, when the shift leads are upstairs counting the money, I sometimes whistle and they sometimes hear me. Only the one with the blonde hair and black dresses can feel me. She wears a cross next to her heart and I think she might be a bit closer to hallowed grounds because of it. I once passed through her body; she trembled, and goose pimples raised on her skin. I flew out of the room, my sheet trailing behind me, laughing all the way to the storage space I've heard them call "The Murder Room", though I think that's a bit insensitive to the dead, but whatever. The irony is, I love that room. I can hear the whir of the projectors rolling, and when the spiders build their webs around the boxes I like to sit and watch them. My only true friends.

They use an area of the upstairs room to throw children's parties, and the kiddies giggle and scream when I dance on the table, dipping my toes into their sodas and cake. It's the only time I really feel alive, but then the kids leave. They go down to their movies, and then, one by one, out the door. When they are gone no one can see me and I kick at the back of old ladies' seats while they cry at the sad indie films and documentaries that no one else watches. After one birthday party, themed after a bright yellow sponge, the parents forgot a sponge-shaped balloon upstairs. The theater workers brought it downstairs to their break room. After a time, it lost some of its air and began floating at face level, so I took it from them and for a while we were inseparable. We had a brief courtship, double featuring horror movies, bobbing along, our feet never touching the ground. It was magic. Until one day I found that she had deflated overnight. The worker with the tall legs and dark brown hair threw her in the trash, and for that, he will never be forgiven. Whenever he works, I climb inside the popcorn machine, rubbing my sheets all over the popping corn, bathing in the coconut oil. Once, I even kicked hard enough to pop off the popcorn machine door and it went clattering to the ground, split into three pieces.

I've been waiting a very long time for someone to die. There is an old man who comes in, grabs a list of the movies showing, then promptly falls asleep in one of them. I sway in front of him, crouch down and check if he is still breathing, and each time, at the end of the movie, he is shaken awake by an employee and I head to the women's bathroom where I flush the toilets while people are sitting on them and have a good cry. That's something that doesn't change when you die. Bathrooms are still the best place for weeping. The violet-haired girl says Moaning Myrtle haunts the toilets. I tried to tell her that it was just me, but I lost my name long ago, and anyways, she only pretends to want to listen. I see how fast she cleans the toilets at night when she knows I'm in there. I'm beginning to think that she really doesn't see me at all. I once tried to push her down the stairs, thought she might look nice in an ivory sheet, her coral high-top tennis shoes poking out underneath, but I was only successful in making her stumble a little. She laughed all the way down the stairs, as if we were playing a funny game. As if I was nothing but a big joke.

I've been waiting so long for someone to spend time with. Then it happened. I was standing beside the violet-haired girl at the counter. I kept tapping her shoe with mine, but she didn't even notice. A man ran up to the counter. "Someone's fallen," he said. She ran out from behind the counter toward the lobby and I floated in her wake. There, on the floor, was an elderly woman, her hair an ashen white. The violet-haired girl bent to her, dipped her head down close to see if the woman was breathing, pressed her hand tentatively to her neck before jumping back, startled at the lack of beating. Behind the woman crumpled on the floor stood a white sheet, black Velcro tennis shoes poking out of the bottom.

I wanted to tell her thank you, thank you for coming here to die, but instead we linked the edges of our sheets where our hands would be and danced a little jig on the patterned carpet. Now, when I stand at the top of the stairs looking out of the mirror there is someone beside me. Each day the violet-haired girl cleans the mirror. I lift one sheet sleeve, then the other, she mimics my moves. My companion tries to copy me, so each day I push her down the stairs. When I sit with the spiders in the murder room there she is. When I haunt the bathroom toilet, she haunts the large handicap stall. She lurks behind me when I dance on the table at the kid's birthday parties.

I'm beginning to wish she hadn't come here to die.

Shiver, Tree Woman

She dreamt about deep winter for months and here it was finally, outside her windows. From the loft of her cabin she could see down to the angular windows that stretched up, up, covering the entire expanse of the cabin wall. The fog, so thick that she couldn't make out anything past the initial row of alders that hid the creek from view. Snow-flakes the size of white powdered donut holes drifted slowly to the ground, past the point where she could see over the lip of the rail. She stuck a precautionary toe outside of her thick plaid comforter to discover that the room was ice. The fire below puttered out while she slept, though she had only slept for maybe four hours and had stoked it thoroughly before climbing the stairs, her mind blissfully blank and ready to give in to sleep. Her hand groped for her plum wool socks on the floor that were removed sometime mid-sleep and pooled together at the bottom of the bed. She slipped them on, launched herself from the safety of her covers, threw on the sweater that hung limp over the desk chair, and made her way down the stairs, almost slipping on the wood coming off the last stair before righting herself and quickly pushing three large chunks of cedarwood from one of the felled trees into the fireplace. Blowing air that came out in puffs of fog from her lips she was able to reignite the coals from the night and the slow creep of warmth pushed out at her.

She crossed to the kitchen, turned on the kettle, and stared out at the blank sheet of gray that looked back from where the forest should be. The snow must have started shortly after she fell asleep, for the ground was covered in a decent layer, though the ferns protruded with marked diligence. If the storm kept up, they would be completely covered by nightfall. Their fronds curled in tight on themselves, waiting, waiting, for the world to melt.

The kettle screeched behind her, reminding her of the sound the wind makes when it whips through the trees. It had been seven years since she and her husband had purchased the cabin deep in the woods between Eugene and the Oregon coast. She poured the steaming water into her cup of blackberry and sage black tea; they had been shown the place by a real estate agent who had all but given up on finding them the perfect home. They arrived twenty minutes before their agent. On the drive out there, off the highway, a left turn onto a dirt road, past an old cemetery where the gravestones were all properly tarnished and old, deeper and deeper into the woods. The houses and farms becoming few and far between the further they drove. Their GPS told them to turn off and they pulled up to the red iron gate. Trevor stepped from the vehicle, typed in the code given to them, and moved the gate slowly to the side before popping back into the driver's seat, driving them far enough on the other side, then getting out again and latching the gate.

It was March, deep into the rainy season, and the water came down in relentless droves. The car eased down the drive, up over the wooden bridge, trundling slowly with care, and around the bend where they popped out into the driveway of the cabin. They had sat in a silence of reverence. The trees rose up around them and everywhere they looked there were lush green beds of moss and twines of ivy swirled around the tree trunks as if in an intimate dance.

When they stepped from the car, she spun a quick circle, arms out, rain bouncing off her teal raincoat, streaking through her long black hair that hung out the sides. Her eyes locked with Trevor's and they broke into a laugh before running and hiding underneath the alcove of the carport.

He pressed her lightly against the wood beams that lined the side of the house and said, "I think we are home."

They found themselves kissing like the teenagers they had previously been, in what seemed like another life, when the agent came into the drive. Two months later they moved into their new home.

It was a drive for Trevor to his job in the city. One he initially said he didn't mind, but later, when the air itself seemed tight and the trees seemed to crowd in and around them it became apparent that she was no longer what he wanted. He couldn't stand her spells of silent contemplation; he no longer understood her blinding euphoria of life or how it could be snubbed out like a lantern's wick for weeks at a time. Now everything was a chore to him: the drive in, the endlessness of cutting wood for the fire, bracing the side of the cabin with sandbags when the rivers poured and sent the creek up to their doorstep in the dead of night, or the way his wife needed equal parts of touch and seclusion. The memory chilled in her, grew cold, and she looked down to discover that her tea, too, was tepid in her hand.

She had left her copy of Brian Doyle's *Mink River*, the spine cracked and the pages peeling away, on the oversized leather chair by the fire. She brought her tea over and curled into a ball, a fleece wrapped tightly around her, the fire crackling, and the silence of snow falling in a wall out the window. She began reading where she left off, felt the characters settle deep into her body, the words pouring through her, "Asin couldn't bear being married or having children or having friends. She ran wild through the woods. If you saw her running you had to run to water as fast as you could and drink or her restlessness would come into you like a thirst that could never be quenched. She was happy and unhappy. She had wild long hair and she was very tall and she ran like the wind. When you saw dunegrass rippling in a line she was running through it. When the wind changed direction suddenly that was Asin. She was never satisfied or content and so she ran and ran and ran." She read for hours, consumed by the need to feel something, anything, in place of this void inside her that had been slowly filling up her body. She was a body thick with sand. Finishing the book for what felt like the hundredth time she discovered the snowfall had broken, if only for a moment. She slipped her socks into her worn boots, flung on her tattered coat, and opened the door into a quiet so deep and all-encompassing she thought, briefly, that maybe she was the only person left on the planet. Maybe that was all there was left, just her and this vast crystallized world. She would be there, forever, trudging through winter.

The thought slipped out as soon as it slipped in, and when she left the stoop her boots made a satisfying crunch under her weight, like walking into a world of styrofoam clouds. She flung herself down into the white froth on the ground and began making a snow angel. Up, down her arms moved in repetition. Out-in, her legs in synchronization. Thump, thump, her heart responded.

"Hello," she said to no one. "Hello!"

Snow fell from a Douglas fir in the distance from the echo of her voice and made a quiet thunk into cushioned ground.

She was relieved, when he left. That's what she hadn't said. In the letters to old high school friends, to her editor who was the closest thing she had to a best friend, to her aging father and her quiet mother. He said he didn't love me anymore, that he couldn't live with a moody poet alone in this god damn house in the middle of nowhere. He needed more. That is what she had written. She hadn't dared write the words, even then, when it was all over—the words she had been dying to say. She thought them, over and over again: *I made him leave, bit by bit, cold shoulder by cold shoulder. I wanted this quiet, the empty nights, a full bed, a life short of demands. I wanted only the looming forest, the snails in the lawn in spring, the deer crossing paths, the wild call of the cougars in heat, the sound of the rain pattering, the sound of my axe slicing into the wood, the sound of no one coming home tired late at night, judging the way I want to live in the world with no business to run to and little love for cleaning or cooking or bursting forth babies from the cavity of my womb.*

The snow angel had stilled. A light dusting of snow touched the tip of her face: she got what she wanted. She always did, in the end. She had wanted Trevor so badly it hurt. It had made her knees shake as she dropped to them for him, when they were just teenagers, just barely out of high school. At the time she would have laid out bare, naked on the cold hard earth, if he had asked her to. She would fuck him anywhere, anytime, her need for him so self-annihilating that to remember that desire was like pressing into a deep bruise. He had been with other girls, before her, and even then, even when she would have given up anything, all of the things, everything she knew, just to feel him touch her one more time, she hadn't cared. Then, when it came time for her to be rid of him, to push his body out of her body, to carve out the lining where she had creased herself into his skin, it was so easy. Everything she needed was already there. She pretended to just be discovering his affairs. The way he tilted his phone from her body when she came near while he sent off a text or one of the hundreds of work emails he claimed. And then one day, when he had come home and she hadn't done anything but write some poems and read, front to back, her copy of *Story Sisters* by Alice Hoffman, she had done it, walked behind him and snatched the phone right out of his hands. It was there, she knew it would be, the words *I can't stop thinking about you.*

It had been so easy, to blow up her life from the inside out. "Pack your bags," she had said.

He'd thrown his duffel in his jeep, then turned to her, "You're pathetic. What the fuck do you think you're going to do? Live out here all alone? You won't last a week without me.

You'll be begging me to come back." He slammed the door and she flipped him off as he peeled out of the drive, up over the old wood bridge creaking under the weight of his car. She couldn't see, but she heard him slam the door shut before cranking out the gate. Yelled *fuck* into the sea of trees at his back as he hopped back in the car, leaving the gate wide open. Later, she walked up to the gate, changed the code on the lock. That was it. After a few months he stopped calling, stopped leaving messages on her voicemail begging her to let him come home, only to call moments later cursing her out calling her a dumb bitch, saying I never loved you anyways.

She hadn't cried.

The snow began flowing from the sky in a river, a full stream. She stood, shook the snow off her, brushed it off the back of her pants, stomped it off her boots at the front door. Opened up. Went in. Shed all her clothes on the rug just inside the door. The windows stared back. *Who was going to see? The crows?*

When she stepped into the steaming shower the scalding water stung every bit of her skin. The pipes rumbled, as if someone were clumsily making their way through the cabin, thumping around the loft above. A haunting. The grant she had received from the university for her poetry would dry up soon. Then what? They owned the house outright, bought with the inheritance her grandfather had left behind at his passing. It was hers to keep. She would win it in the divorce, should there ever be a divorce. She couldn't imagine being confronted by Trevor's face. His cool, green eyes. The look with its old, deep hunger.

The scalding water made her body feel feral. This body, which sometimes felt like hers and other times felt apart from her. A remembered body. A past. A body with a life of its own. She no longer felt desire. Not in the waking hours. She wanted only to read her books, to walk among the trees, follow the curving line of the creek up into the mountains, follow it back down to the cabin. But her body had other ideas. In the night, in her sleep, she was a sensual creature. Her body something very old. A mountain lion. She imagined that when she slept her body sizzled, that steam rose off her skin in puffs of smoke.

The water poured over her face and she grasped for the marker on the top of the white board that she kept at the back of the shower where the water droplets wouldn't reach.

She scribbled down,

> *Shiver, tree women,*
>
> *Violent against desire.*
>
> *Thrashing in the wake of*
>
> *Thirst.*

Empty river.

Her editor would like that one, she thought. Something to tide her over. Let her know that, yes, she could create again, would create again. Yes.

She stepped from the shower, groped for a towel and found none.

"Shit."

She stumbled out to the kitchen, dripping water all over the hardwood floors. The heat from the fire barely warmed this part of the cabin. At the linen closet she reached in for a clean towel, only to find none.

"Fuck!"

Naked, goose bumps rose across her skin, she walked to the kitchen and found a small hand towel in the drawer. She dried herself, bit by bit, stark in front of the window of snow that hung itself delicately outside the alcove of greenhouse-shaped windows of the dining area. Part window wall, part ceiling. As she wrung out her thick hair, she looked out into the creeping winter darkness. Her stomach rumbled harshly, notifying her that she had, indeed, forgotten to eat today. As she reached the tips of her hair, crinkling and rubbing the towel around them loosely she noticed a body slinking slowly from the footpath she often took up into the trees. The beige body almost, but not quite, blending in with the snow. Shoulders thick with fur slinked, rippled, rolled, as the cougar made its way down, down, down the hill towards her. Its golden eyes pierced her. The towel dropped from her hand and she stepped toward the cool touch of the glass on her body. The window felt sheer, an invisible curtain between her and the magnificent creature only feet from her. Her vulnerability didn't concern her. She slid the glass door open.

The cougar froze. Its paw so large it could cover her face. Knock her back with one swat. She stepped, naked and bare footed, into the crisp blinding light of snow.

Snow landed clumped onto the wild cat's fur and the ground, the ferns, the trees, all. The creek was rushing off through the deeper woods. The sensation of pleasure rippled through her. Slight, at first, and then uncontrollably. Her heart pumped ferociously in her chest. The cougar's chest moved inconceivably slow, stilled by the snow.

The cat turned from her, looped back towards the path where it had come from. It turned, gave her one last look, blinked. Slow. Languid. It scampered up into the trees, out of sight.

She stepped out into the yard, the snow past her chilled ankles. She came to the spot where the cougar had stood. She bent and pressed her palm down into the footprint. It felt warm.

She hadn't felt this alive in years. Something burst open inside of her. A locked cellar. A dried up well. It filled, overflowed, burgeoned out around her.

The snow stopped, abruptly. A cloud moved past her in the sky. A redolent blue crept out of the edges, tinted by the magenta of day ending. She heard the fireplace crackling, dying behind her.

Grizzly

Nearly all the lights were on, each illuminated window a portion of his life that wasn't hers. No movement appeared in the front; no bodies in the space between the window frames. She crept around to the back of the house, where the house pressed against the edge of the woods.

The blackberry vines were thick with ripe berries. She felt clumsy like a grizzly bear, stumbling along, hands grasping at branches like paws, biting down on her tongue.

Her intention wasn't to be seen; it was to see.

She plucked an overripe blackberry and pressed it to her lips, bruising them purple. She dropped the crushed berry to the ground, then crouched behind a fresh cut pile of firewood, and peered over the top of the pile into his office. The desk faced the window. Behind it, against the far wall in the dark, were the perfectly dusted spines of books like Tolstoy and Shakespeare, books he never read but thought he should own; the old books she'd felt against her chest where he had pinned her to the wall. She imagined the hard surface of the desk against her back.

The scratch of a record player cut through. A *Sunday Kind of Love* shimmered and echoed. The disturbance knocked her off kilter and tipped the top log off the pile, knocked the axe to the ground. Her reflection stared up from the sheen of the blade, dark brown hair frazzled; her face unrecognizable.

A shadow passed the backdoor. A movement down the hall, the silhouette of the woman's sunshine hair—a halo against the forest green walls, wandered out towards the darkness.

Just the sight of the woman triggered a deep pit in her stomach.

She used to be what he did on Thursday nights, but had been replaced by this fox of a woman, smaller, sly. A nuisance, at best.

Her shoulders tensed as if they were growing, expanding, stretching out of the confines of her dress.

The woman stepped outside the back door in her bare feet, dumped a bowl of food in the compost, humming along with the music.

She stepped around the woodpile; her mouth opened wide.

The woman paused, feeling the hot air on her neck. The woman turned quickly in a circle. There was no one, only a flicker at the edge of her vision. A clump of fur tangled in the brambles, tangled in her hair.

She thought the woman's hair was blonde, the shine of dandelions held up to pale skin, but maybe it was brown? There was no longer humming. She stared into the woods. A mirage in the dusk reflected something back at her she wished she'd never seen.

He was pulling into the driveway. He was whistling. He threw his keys on the side table inside the house and tipped his face into the vase full of sunflowers, breathing in slowly. The record player scratched off the track, cut to silence.

Down the hall, the shadows of twilight looked like deep grooves dashed down the sides of the freshly painted walls. He called for his wife, then stepped into his backyard. Cricket thoraxes formed a chorus of vibrations in the air.

Something glistened in the dual image. He turned to find his wife's ring on the blackberry vine and plucked the diamond, as if it was ripe and his to keep.

Deer-Hearted

-1-

It isn't that she wants to recapture her youth, but that she can't escape it. It is the drip, drip, drip from the bathroom ceiling vent that leaks into the pot on the bathroom floor every time it rains. Her husband has searched tirelessly for the leak for many years, becoming incensed up on the roof in the pouring rain looking for the place where the water gets in. Every time he is up there, the phrase, "the dam will not hold" ricochets around her head, though she isn't sure where it comes from or why.

She will be turning 40 this year and she finds life has gotten more and more like that, nonsensical, predictable. The mystery has evaporated, had it ever really been there, and the writing is no longer coming the way it used to, ushering in like a thrashing wind, electric. She still reads voraciously, that hasn't changed, though some are prone to thinking that all this reading is a cover-up for what she will not admit or address. Though what exactly that is, her friends did not know—they could hazard a guess.

Every time she sits down to write, words come out, but they don't feel like hers. Whose hand is this aching? She feels her bottom cradled in her worn out chair and re-reads the words, wondering if they really are hers, or maybe they belong to someone else, something she had read somewhere else once. Everything feels derivative. She has become a carbon copy of something: a lonely white woman in her small home, whittling away her days, returning to the same material of her youth again and again to slate her cloying hunger. The thought of herself, her life, a cliché from half the books on the best sellers list, revolts her.

She tears the paper from her notebook, crumples it, and tosses it toward the trash can where the ever growing pile of crumpled papers grows inside and around.

"For fucks sakes," she speaks to the empty attic room.

Even her beloved writing room which she had painstakingly curated to be equal parts cozy and academic, the first room in the house she set up when they moved in, feels like someone else's. Like a room from every movie set ever created for the character of *the writer*: mahogany desk centered, bookshelves bursting, and large windows staring back at the writer, wasting away the hours on a pursuit that makes less and less sense to her as time goes on.

Pushing away from the desk, she laces her fingers and stretches toward the wooden beams that race across the unfinished ceiling, leaning one way first and then the other. Her tea grown cold, she picks it up, cupping it between her palms, and crosses to the window. Her breath creates fog on the pane and with one cold finger she traces out an old and forced to be forgotten name before rubbing her sweater sleeve over it in a violent swipe, terrified of herself, of who she can still become. Her toes ache from the cold of the attic, despite the wool socks, and she flexes them back and forth, trying to create sensation.

It's late autumn and nearly all the trees are bare, staring at her, stark and empty in her tower. November is always to blame, ushering in the darkness, desolate and already creeping at the outermost edges of the lawn where the forest waits in quiet trepidation for the predators to awake and roam. The rain falling in concurrent droves stills time, a static channel. Suddenly, something shoots out from the shadow of the trees, landing swift and gracefully into the bright-blue bird bath at the center of the lawn. Blinking rapidly and rubbing her eyes, she tries to figure out if her lack of sleep and imagination is playing tricks on her, but no, there in the waning light a small grey hawk stands statuesque in the center of the bird bath, filled to the brim with rain water. Unblinking in its feral beauty, an intense desire overcomes her and she rushes down the stairs, slips her feet into her mustard yellow rain boots, and yanks open the sliding glass doors.

As soon as the trundling sound of her boots smashing down the stairs starts, the hawk catapults into the sky, its wing span impressive, all sharp angles. It darts away as quickly as it arrived, and in her stomach, she feels forlorn, deserted by a great love. Still, she steps down into the squelching grass, boots becoming instantly mud-lined. By the time she reaches the bird bath, her sweater is already soaked. She stares down into the water, willing the hawk to reappear. She needs to see the cool gaze of its eyes. She wants to pluck them out and swallow them. But there is nothing there but her reflection wavering in the ripples on the surface like a hologram. Not quite real. She swipes her hand through the water sending it spraying out the sides of the bath, dashing her likeness away.

For a brief moment, she had felt something, but now the moment has already passed. Here she is again, hollow in all the wrong places. Bird bones. She stares into the ever-darkening woods, only finally shaken out of her reverie by the lumbering sounds of her husband's truck coming down the drive.

-2-

She had first tried to write about her youth while she was in it. Deep in the muck of the belly of that particular beast, adolescence. All that impetuous craving: thighs, hands, tongues thick with desire. Seventeen and so in love, no thing so sublimely unnerving as young love in a dying coastal town. It wasn't essay or story that she turned to then, how could it be? Those forms better suited for the heavy fog of loss, which comes for us all eventually. No, it was poetry she turned to. Rancid, rhyming, unseasoned and volatile in its staggering badness. But what else was there? How else to describe that particular heat when you're in it?

She could still recall a few lines, though she hesitated to do so. How could she have ever been so young? The relationship that had defined her teenage years was long and painful, not one single part of it anything but a tragedy; a reckless, violent force of nature that ripped through town, leaving no aspect of her body untouched. She had gone to her knees for that love and she was on her knees still, palms muddied crying in the dirt, head bobbing between his legs, on her knees snorting a line off a dollar bill held taut in his hands, on her knees with him behind her, on her knees pleading, sometimes for more, sometimes the *no, no, no* of it still wrong in her mouth.

-3-

She steps through the back door of their house as her husband steps through the front. He slides his work boots over the bristled rug, scraping the muck off them before he looks up and notices her. Her sweater drips rivulets of rain onto the hardwood and the sound is what pulls his attention as he drops his lunch pail by the door.

"What are you doing?" he looks at her incredulously.

She bunches the pastel pink of her sweater in her hands, ringing the edges out on the floor.

"There was a hawk in the bird bath."

"What?"

"A hawk. I saw it cut from the trees and land in the bird bath."

She slips her soaked feet out of her rain boots, strips the wool socks from her feet, and looks down at her body, as if she isn't sure how she got inside it.

"But why are you soaked?" he pulls out a chair from the table and the scrape of the leg on the floor seems to reverberate through the whole house. A haunting. He unlaces his boots systematically, not looking up.

"Well, I wanted to get a better look, but it flew away once I was out there and it was raining really hard."

She pulls her sweater over her head and it lands on the floor with a plop. She crosses to the fireplace and stokes it, holding her hands out to the flames, the bright red of her fingertips like cigarette embers glowing. He crosses to her, her back toward him, and the pale yellow of her bra looks fragile across the canvas of her spine. He puts his arms around her waist, her skin clammy from the cold.

"So did you just stand out there in the rain?"

She shrugs.

"Are you sure it was even a hawk? What would a hawk be doing in the bird bath when it's pouring rain?"

She bristles, pulling away from him, her eyes the cool glaze of the bird.

"It was a fucking hawk," she says, her tone clipped, but unsure why she is so angered by his question, "I know what I saw."

He holds up his hands, like waving a white flag. She doesn't say another word, just heads up the stairs and follows them to the glow of the lamp at the top. On each step is the wet imprint of her feet trailing after her. She strips in her office, depositing the soaked clothes by the door, and grabs her mother's afghan from the back of the leather couch. She pulls it over her shoulders like a cape, picks up her pen, and stares at the blank page before her. The chill of her body makes her feel alert, like she's in her skin.

-4-

When she was ten her grandmother died. She knew it before she knew it—her mom home from work on lunch break, watering the wildflower seeds she had scattered in the front garden box that had blossomed into the most brilliant shades of jewels and sunsets. Her mother collapsed, her calf-length pink dress ballooned out around her, shoulders hunched and shaking. She looked like a cupcake on a beautiful summer day, but the cordless phone was dangling from her hand limply and tears rolled down her face.

She'd never seen her mom cry, not even once, and this is how she knew that something was terribly wrong before she was told. Her and her siblings watched her mom from the dining room window, separated by a pane of glass and an experience that only time can hold.

Years later, she would discover her grandmother had wanted to be a writer, but there's was a large family, a working-class family. She spent her days rearing her children, caring for their house and their land. Her grandmother had kept a journal, and when she died it was discovered that she had collected all the letters back from the recipients she had sent them to. A living archive of her dreams, her thoughts, her worries.

All she can really recall about that summer and the funeral now is the sweltering heat, the way the blue and black plaid striped sweater and skirt set itched her skin as she sat in the grass at her mom's feet, clutching her little brother, while the pastor spoke above the box she refused to look into that now held her grandmother's lifeless body.

She remembers the brick siding of her great grandmother's house, how it looked at dusk as she peered through the window at her family, an outsider looking in, unable to process grief in a normal way, hiding her body under the towering lilac bush in the yard. The scent of lilacs so heady that all her life when the aroma reaches her nose she will find herself again under her great grandmother's lilac bushes, watching her older sister pass through the kitchen on the other side of the window, her long dark brown hair so like their mothers, held off her face with a scarf.

-5-

It seems to her that nobody writes about what happens in the years after someone leaves an abusive relationship: how it alters you, how you hold your body different, how your body no longer seems to hold you. So often they write about the relationship, they write about escaping it, or worse, the terrible things that happen when someone doesn't escape, when they never get their narrow miss.

She's lying in bed, woken by the sound of the screen door slapping closed, the rattle of her husband's truck firing up as he leaves for work. The wind is violent today. Everything trembles and shakes. The rose bush outside their bedroom window—which she keeps forgetting to trim down for the winter—no longer producing buds, scratches at the glass with each gust. The noise, like fingernails on glass, feels like it's deep inside her skull, coming from within. So many things feel like an attack, bombarding her senses.

Her husband is a good man. And she doesn't mean "good, but…" He's actually a good man. He's calm. He yields. He's gentle, never yells, doesn't try to manipulate her, to pressure her, never makes demands, not even for love when she has none to give. It's a kind of madness, his form of quiet loyal devotion. To her, it seems a madness. She is not gentle. She is harsh, moody and hungry and desperate and often unyielding. It becomes impossible to yield when your body did it for so many years, broke its back for someone else, it no longer bends that way, the spine stiff, no curve. It does not break.

The wind hushes and in the silence a rush of crows lift from the towering trees in the distance. Their calls ricochet through the sky and she tilts her head on the pillow, watches them fly overhead. She rises from the bed, grabbing her robe off the hook, and pads out to the kitchen. The counters have been wiped clean and the coffee pot is still on. Her favorite mug left sitting beside it. The sight of it there sends a pang through her side, like swimming right after eating. It's been fifteen years, she thinks, how is he still not done loving me yet?

-6-

When she was 19-years-old she found herself upended. She had left the boy, the one with all the anger and the steely-blue eyes, the cobra-heart. The idea for the first book came then, the one she'd never finish writing. A memoir of her exploits. She would write it in secret, while her new boyfriend, the one with the dark brown curly hair and the wild laugh was out fishing on the Columbia River. In between her full-time retail job. In between the lines of oxy she had taken to snorting to survive those last few years with someone who made himself impossible to continue to love. In between fucking her new boyfriend and weeping while they did it and him pleading, *what's wrong, what's wrong, what's wrong*. In between all that, she began the memoir titled *I Was Crazy Too*, not yet ready to absolve herself from what was done to her and the things she did in return to survive it. Not yet able to understand that she wasn't crazy, what she was was abused, was traumatized, was desperately alive. That crazy was a word lined up like the 8-ball at the end of a round of billiards, shot straight at her with enough force to send her reeling. Lobbed like a molotov cockatil.

She wrote the beginning of the love story and then hid it under the seat of her car where no one would find it. It wasn't until years later, reading *Wuthering Heights* for the first time, when she found herself livid that the world marketed this book as one of the greatest love stories ever told, that she saw the lie, first of Heathcliff as an unruly narcissist masked as a great love, then her own love story, which was also not a love story, but instead a story of great despair.

The story she thought she had been writing crumpled before her. It was obsession, bright and blistering and cold as a winter's night. It was anguish and loneliness and cruelty masquerading as romance. There had been love in it, but it was a calculating sort of love, a love with checks and balances, devious. It wasn't the kind of love that brought you to your knees, it was the kind that forced you there.

-7-

She's wandering the woods, his hand pressed tightly in hers. Earlier, they kissed under the bough of a large autumn tree, crimson leaves falling down and the whole world mired in fog. They make their way over a bridge, dangling precariously low to the rushing water below it. Suddenly, they are separated. It's pitch black out. She grows cold. She calls his name, screams it, but only the tumultuous crash of the river below answers.

She wakes, her mouth rounded in the shape of his name. It is a name she doesn't speak in her waking life, hasn't spoken in years for what the sound of it will resurrect into the air. Her eyes snap open. A breathless "oh" escapes and sends a puff of air into the silence as she discovers herself out deep in the woods behind her house. Wet pine needles press into the pads of her feet and the sharpness of the cold is a buoy to the rising panic.

Turning, she sees the glow of a dim light in the distance, barely illuminating the trail she must have followed in her sleep. She looks around in search of ghosts or other devils hidden between the trees, half expecting the silhouette of her past love to slink his way from behind a trunk, or come up behind her, sliding his hands around her waist, dipping below the elastic of her pajama pants, a man with strawberry blonde hair and flashing eyes greedy with the hunger she can still taste.

An owl hoots in the distance and the snap of a twig sends her heart hammering. A fawn, the back half brown and the front a dewy white, as if from a different world, steps out across the trail between her and the house. They both freeze, locking eyes. The cold night air sends tremors between them, in the deer's gaze she feels naked with recognition, like it can see all her harbored selves. Her desire is there, where it's always humming, between the lining of her throat, her lungs hammering as she swallows, deer-hearted. When it finally turns and darts into the trees, the bubble bursts and she is just a woman, cold and alone in the woods, chasing ghosts.

She steps gingerly, following the trail to her own back door and the life she built. Unlatching the door quietly and shutting it gently behind her, she is greeted by the last crackles of their dying fire and the light snores of her husband drift down the stairs. The terror from finding herself, a walking nightmare in the woods, makes her shiver where she stands in the dark of her kitchen. Surrounded by her own possessions—ones she carefully picked out, curated, placed around her house like a little museum to who she wanted to be—seem strange to her on this weird November night. Goose bumps rise like a tidal wave across her skin and she crosses to the stove, cranking the burner knob until the gas ignites and a flame flickers.

The chamomile warms her as she stands over their farmhouse sink looking out the window and wondering what would have happened to her if she kept up the dream and chased her old love through the woods all night. There's an ache in the pit of her stomach. She feels she is still out there now, calling his name, that she has been out there all along, all these years. It shames her, this desire.

By the time she crawls back under the warmth of their winter quilt, dawn is creeping up the sides of the house, trying to get into the windows. Her husband rolls over, waking to the almost light. He is unaware of her departure, unaware of so many things. Unaware of who she used to be, who she still is now, here under the blankets beside him, who she becomes on the page or in the dark. He wishes he would feel it, her absences like that of a wound, the way she learned to love all those years ago. But he is not that kind of man, and that is not this kind of love. He doesn't obsess. He doesn't strangle or suffocate—though sometimes she wishes he would, just to conjure up the old feeling. She sometimes feels held by the quiet enduring love of his, yet other times it is a canyon between them and she is choking on the clear air.

He rises to shower and she keeps her back toward him, her eyes blinking against the rise of the dream as he pads to the bathroom and clicks on the light. The rush of the water starting draws her eyelids down and she doesn't wake again until the sky has already turned from pink to yellow to blue. He's long gone down the drive. The house is empty. All that's left is the cloying scent of Marlboro reds in the air, though neither of them smoke, and the gnawing sensation that she awoke something in the dark.

Pane

She lies in bed, the early hours of dawn whispering around her. The January light streams through the window and the empty branches of the maple tree, shifting from midnight to pale-egg blue. The pressure of her lips, one on top of the other, feel heavy. The migraine of yesterday pulses in the back of her temple. Her short blond hair spikes up around her skull giving her the look of a woman overly familiar with long white gowns and electroshock therapy. *Maybe, if I just stay here all day, watching the change of light.* Groping around the nightstand, she clicks on the lamp. Squints at the illumination. Cranking her lighter she sparks a joint and burrows back under the plaid duvet. The smoke twists up into the shadow of the room. *I am a whisper of unfurling smoke.* She opens a book of poetry but doesn't read the words, just stares out the window wondering why the migraines have returned now that she's home. The ceiling fan clicks tirelessly above.

He sits at a table in the corner of the bar overlooking the river, feels the slap of the waves inside him as he sips his beer. His thick clumsy fingers peel at the damp label on the bottle. Out the window, the soft green of the bridge, the orange of the sunset, and the glistening gold of the water greet him. He doesn't think about his brother, out in the water past the bar, the waves rising above the edge of the boat, pummeling his tender cheeks while he reels in the net. Doesn't think of the needles that his brother puts into his arms. He doesn't think of his father's small and violent body drifting on the seabed. Doesn't think about the sound the hull of a ship makes as it's ripped in two or the silence it makes on the bottom of the ocean. A waiter comes and collects his empty bottle, replaces it with a full one without asking. They share a nod. A sea lion lifts its head from the river tide, stares at the man through the window, his black eyes unblinking. Lifting its head, it yells out into the swirling grey clouds rolling in from the west, blotting out the summer sky.

They board a flight set for California. *11A, 12A, 13A* they count, stopping at 14A and pointing at the person in 14B at the window seat. They shove their backpack under the seat ahead of them and stare out the smudged window above the wing, waiting for the slow leave. They didn't expect it to hurt so much, the leaving. It was their choice, after all. The fight they'd had was the kind you never come back from, where the things that get said can never be forgotten. The California coast had been home, once, but they had since grown accustomed to the flat plains for miles and miles, the view of the blue mountaintops in the distance, the feel of their partner's arms around them, staring out into the collapsed silence of 4 am, the quiet moment before they set out to take care of the animals on their small farm. Looking down at their chipped pink nails against the brown of their skin, they wonder who will put the chickens in the coop on nights when no one is home. The plane begins to move backwards. *I am a flightless bird with stretched out wings.* Then, the trundling below as they race to meet the sky. The horizon meets them with its early morning glow before ascending through the clouds. The Tetons rise up around them, then disappear under the belly of the plane.

She stands before the open window above the kitchen sink. The smell of spring wafts through the screen as her thin fingers sift through the sink full of dishes, hands alighting on the pieces of silverware. She tosses them into the empty basin; the sharp clank momentarily blots out the sound of the birds. An orb weaver builds a web from the eave of the house on the other side of the screen. She is startled when arms envelope her waist and the bristled hair of her partner's beard tickles her ear. Brushing her long crimson hair behind her ear, he kisses the side of her head. She watches him walk into the other room before turning her attention back to the spider. *I am not in love with you*, she thinks. The spider builds with precision. Closing her eyes, she thinks about the man she made love to on a cold January night in New England, imagines his thin body against the cool white sheets; it had felt as though the snow outside fell through the ceiling and all around them. A line of geese cross overhead through the sky. She pulls the plug from the sink and looks at her hands, which are shriveled from the lukewarm water.

He climbs the stairs to his second-floor apartment, turns the key in the door. He crosses the room and pulls up the blinds on the window. It is 3 am and the spell of night in winter has been cast. He kicks on the record player, moves the spindle to the fourth ring and listens for the scratch as Leonard Cohen's "Famous Blue Raincoat" rises into the room. The snow flurries around the streetlights. He removes his shoes and socks. A tabby cat slinks out of the bedroom and winds through his ankles. He scratches behind the cat's ears before removing his coat and draping it on a wicker chair. The snow dances around the street; he stands hypnotized by the motion, mindlessly unbuttons his shirt: one, two, three, four, five. Pulling his arms from the sleeves, the cat mewls at his feet. He sits down on his leather couch; the cool texture kisses his skin. He grabs the end of the wrap that compresses his chest, unspools it slowly. Releases the pressure with one slow breath and grabs the afghan throw from the back of the couch. He covers his body like a cloak. He lies down on his side, the cat pooled at his feet. From this vantage point the snowflakes look like they are pummeling him. *I'm a winter king in a winter world*, he thinks as he drifts off to sleep.

They lie in bed watching the January light dance around them. A tabby cat hops up, pools around the arc of their feet. The smudged window makes the world hazy and quiet filters around them while memory trundles through them. A line of geese calls out somewhere. A spider builds a web in the corner. They reach for the empty glass on the nightstand, wishing there was someone around to refill it. Holding the glass, they stare blankly into the cool blue of January. They feel the pressure of their lips, one on top of the other, their chest tight, their elbows crunched, as if they had been trapped for hours in the belly of a plane, jutted up against a room full of strangers. Their hands feel shriveled from age, their skin loose as if a body underwater. *I am alive*. Their eyes shutter. *I am*. The heavy curtain of winter night descends.

Each day she sits in the same spot on the dark green couch, sunken into the corner cushions. From here she can turn her head and look out at the tall stalks of red roses on the other side of the front window, blooming in the blossoming June heat. Mostly, she stares out the sliding back door. The tall un-mowed grass reaches its nimble fingers around the hammock, the patio, the firepit, the wooden bench. Small birds visit the feeder, and she names them out loud. Keeping a record no one will see or remember. "Dark Eyed Junco. House Finch. Black Capped Chickadee. Lesser Goldfinch. House Sparrow." At the bird bath: "Crow. Crow. Crow." A cool breeze rustles the branches of the trees. *How would it feel?* The sun. The wind. Suddenly, she's at the door, sliding it open along its tracks. Stepping out onto the cool pavement of the cement patio, the glass removed, she wiggles her toes. *There is nothing separating me and the world*, she thinks. A thrumming pounds around her and she clutches her heart, eclipsed by a moment of panic when she thinks the noise is coming from inside. "Anna's Hummingbird," she whispers when she sees the emerald green back glistening in the sun, the neon pink neck pumping wildly, beak burrowed into the flowers dangling from the fuchsia plant. It darts over towards her tangled pale hair, imagining the locks to be another source of pollen. It zips away, up into the sky, and she watches it fly away. *I am a body of light with a sunflower head.* She takes a few more steps away from the sliding glass door.

Pigeon House

I wake in my queen size bed. I lace my fingers behind my head before opening my eyes. I know what awaits me on the other side of my lids, a room filled with pigeons and an empty spot beside me. The dream I was having felt too real to want to pull myself out of it. William stood across from me in an empty parking lot outside of our dodge neon. We were disagreeing about something, and I said "I've loved you since I was fifteen. I'm thirty-one now. I've loved you over half my life and I'm not going to stop now." He moved toward me, his hand outstretched, and that's when I woke, and now I press my eyes tightly, sealing them like a jar, trying to push away the light. It was the shuffling of wings that pulled me out of it, just as William and I were about to kiss.

It's not the morning light streaming through the window above the bed that blinds me, but a hundred sets of tiny orange eyes blinking back into the daylight from the floor, the bottom of the bed frame, the dresser, the chair that sits in the corner. Their heads bobble and small crooning noises erupt as, one after another, the pigeons notice I am awake.

Whooo, whooo. The whispers of a hundred pigeons take flight inside my body and I feel myself levitate into the air and open up my wings. But just as easily, I sink back down into the yawning mouth of the bed. Flight was never my dream. It was William's. That's why the birds are here. They're trying to tell me that William is dead. That William is a bird. That he'll never come back to me. But I don't listen. I won't listen. I will not let him fly from me.

I stretch out my arms and toes and accidentally tap the protruding purple chest of a wide-set bird atop my metal bed frame. He shuffles away and emits what is akin to a huff.

"Well, you shouldn't make a home on people's heads."

I rise from the nest of my down white comforter and tiptoe across the hard-wood floor, weaving between birds, wings all aflutter. *And with one swoop of her hand Lily parted the grey sea.* After checking my slippers for birds and poop I slip my toes into them and head across the room to light a fire. It's only early November but already the chill on the coast is so volatile in the morning that I'm suspicious a snow could fall within the week. A small purple pigeon is nestled into the wood stack and I pick her up the way you would a baby rabbit and set her gently down next to me, her eyes enamored at the growth of the flames.

I hear the gentle tap of a hundred claws making their way down the hallway. They are usually polite enough not to fly inside. When I turn from the wood burning stove delicate wobbling heads have pressed in all around, as if I, no, the stove, were their leader. A hush falls over the room as they warm themselves by the fire. It feels like applause.

I shuffle through their bodies and peek out the front window. The old ladies are out in matching track suits. They look like crinkly versions of Power Rangers, except instead of saving the world they are dedicated to saving the neighborhood and to do so they have aimed all their powers of will at getting the crazy pigeon lady out and leveling her pigeon house. They whisper among themselves and cast vicious looks my way, their eyes become teeth. Only a few short months ago, I was just their sweet, young librarian who lived with her handsome blue-eyed husband on the corner of Pleasant Avenue.

But I guess that's how fast the world can turn on you. Close your eyes and fall asleep and when you wake up the man you love is no longer there beside you. He becomes a figment, a ghost, and next thing you know; your house is swarmed with pigeons. It starts small. At first just a few birds in the trees. Their haunting little whoos whispering down at you. But then more and more come. Soon they're on your porch, nesting in your shed, destroying your garden. And then, finally, one day, you look up and they are in your house. But I don't need to tell you this. You already know the way that love can turn fowl.

William and I were still newlyweds the first time it happened, barely two months in. It was night and he had been out late. I don't know where he had been. After our wedding he became distant. He wasn't always the charismatic and bristling young man I married or that I'd been in love with for two years. I had noticed small things before the wedding, little changes I didn't read too much into: dark circles under his eyes, the way he'd tilt his cell phone away from my body at an angle so I couldn't see the screen. His body seemed taut like a livewire at times, and other times he was languid and heavy.

On this night, I noticed the pallor of his skin. He came into the room and began undressing me without a word. No *Hello, baby.* His eyes seemed black even though they were actually ice blue, and I felt the stare acutely, the way a woman walking alone on a darkened street feels when she knows there is someone behind her. I tried to kiss him, but he pushed my face away. He wasn't after love making. There was something else inside him. A beast. A monster. When it was over, he lay beside me gulping for air. He said my name, at first like it was a curse, then a whisper, then a cry.

Over the following years the cavern in my stomach grew larger, with each turn of his head. He no longer looked to me like the man I had fallen in love with. Where his eyes had been kind and clear they were now cloudy and narrow, as if he were looking for something that wasn't there, things that only existed in his mind. They were steely and cool and unmoving. His nose grew pointier as his face grew skinnier. I felt small and wild against the abstraction of him.

"I want to be a bird in the afterlife," he once said to me on a good day. We had been at the beach and I had packed a picnic and brought along my parents' old wool blanket to sit on. It was August and the sun shone through his curly hair and lit up his smile.

"Why a bird?" I had asked.

He looked out toward the waves, eyes settling on a far-away point that I couldn't see, like the green light on the dock in Fitzgerald's Gatsby.

"All that freedom," he said: "They've got the whole wide world around and below them."

He shook the seriousness from his eyes.

"Let's build a sandcastle." He jumped up and raced away toward the dark, wet sand.

I looked around at the pigeons wondering if one was him, but maybe what he wanted most he could never become.

***

Lily woke in her queen size bed. She was late for work at the coffee shop, and even though she was the owner, late was late. She threw on an oversized grey sweater and a pair of yesterday's stiff jeans, she flew down the stairs, out the door, and down the front porch. Birds ricocheted into the sky as her body propelled into the world. A storm of pigeons, startled by the quick movement where previously the world had been silent as if covered in a thick blanket, swirled and turned over their purple-grey bodies in the sky.

Lily watched as they catapulted up into the air, out, only to calmly land again, one after the other, on her sinking lichen covered roof, the maple tree, the porch railing, in the garden, on the shed, on a sunflower, a trowel that had fallen to the side and lay covered in a layer of grime and moss, on the brick pavers, her mailbox, the fence, and on her car. She had forgotten. Forgotten what she had become. She was the lady who lived in the Pigeon House. The one with the missing husband whose daughter lay up in her room across the hall on the second floor. The one about whom people whispered as she passed.

No one came into the Latte Library anymore. There was no use going to work or opening up the shop or doing anything other than sitting in the bay window and watching as more and more pigeons came in to roost, to fill up her yard, to fall into the cavern at the center of her heart. The hole left when he left or disappeared or died. A man was there and then he was not and the only thing left was pigeons and a daughter who was relieved that the bad man was gone, even though the bad man used to be a good man, used to be a man that you couldn't stop loving.

Making her way back up the porch stairs and into the house, her body moved like it was walking through mud. Her steps were heavy, her mind blank, empty as a summer's day, except it wasn't summer and her hope didn't spring eternal. It was dead and he was dead, she was sure of it. Why else would the birds be here? She found herself standing at the kitchen window, looking out at the frothing Pacific Ocean that thrashed on the other side.

How did I get here? she thought, *How did I become this woman?*

The warbling reached her ears and she turned to look behind her. In horror she'd realized she'd forgotten to close the door. The grey and purple bobbing bodies of a hundred birds thrummed around her like an orchestra of drums. They landed on chairs, made themselves comfortable on the ratty sofa, found their way into baskets and bookcases and stood alight on the top of the tea kettle, peering at her with unblinking eyes.

"Get out," she whispered, and then: "Get out!" she shouted. But the pigeons didn't move. She was the pigeon keeper, after all. Lily had no say in the matter. She'd been cursed. Perhaps she *was* the curse.

The birds. They were everywhere.

Lily looked around at the birds alight on every surface, covering the floors with the tiny scritches of tiny feet.

"Amy," Lily called up the stairs, "You've got to come see this."

But no sound came from upstairs. For there was no one there. No daughter. No husband. There was nothing but silence in her big old house by the sea. Silence and the empty sound of bird's eyes, staring back at her, unblinking.

***

You wake up in your queen size bed. You know what awaits you on the other side of your lids sewn closed by the lorazepam sleep. Those damn fucking birds. They aren't even real, you know that, or at least you think you know that. But here they are all the same. He always told you he wanted to be reincarnated as a bird. It's kind of ironic that he came back as a pigeon because they mate for life and he couldn't keep it in his fucking pants, not with you and not with anyone who saw the cool blue eyes set in a face with strict and unforgiving lines. You were just the only one willing to ignore his lies.

You open your eyes and, sure as shit, there they are. Their empty orange eyes blink back at you. Pigeons roosting on every open space. A fucking sea of pigeons and you feel like you're in the nut house, but you're not. You're in your own home that's covered in pigeons both inside and out. That it could come to this. Not the birds—no one could anticipate the birds—but what happened before the birds.

You'd see those women on the street, the bird ladies: you'd never be one of them. Their hands like delicate fluttering paper, body tight and thin and reed small. They look like they could blow away, like the slightest touch would send the pieces of them scattering, up into the sky. Like antique mirrors. Fragile and used and left uncared for by the thoughtless hands of men who stared through them. That's what you had thought. *Never, ever. That won't happen to me.* But here it has passed. Suddenly your house is like something out of a Kafka novel. And you, from a Marquez story, the very old woman with enormous wings. But your wings are not enormous. It's just that there are so many of them.

You pass through the sea of birds. You scream and they lift from their perches and hover in the air. Then they settle back down. In the window there it is: your reflection. A bird lady. There are feathers in your hair. William's boots sit by the front door and you stick your feet in them. Your plaid pajamas bunch up around your calves and spill over the top of the boots.

You're like one of the fishermen out at the piers, sweatpants bagged up around their extra tuff's, hair raggedy and frazzled. *Fresh off the boat*, you think, back from the relentless tumult of the sea.

Outside a young girl runs past the house. Her hair is in long black braids, and you remember when you used to wear your long pale hair plaited. William thought it was magnificent, and then he made you cut it because he didn't like the way that other men looked at you.

The girl's thighs move with such grace. She could be a dancer. You walk down the steps and out into the yard.

"Hello," you call out and your throat catches, as if you're choking on feathers. She doesn't hear you and you don't try again.

But she stops anyway and looks up at you. It's your appearance, or maybe it's all these birds. Then she turns from your house and begins to run again, her long hair flapping behind her and the sound of her shoes slapping the pavement reverberates through your spine.

You whisper, "He won't leave me alone."

***

I imagine that I am a pigeon. I examine the delicate wings of the one nesting on my lap like a cat or a small dog, its feet tucked under its protruding grey stomach. The afternoon light casts an iridescent glimmer over the wings. They look like an oil spill, metallics running through them. I look down at the frayed tips of my long and tangled hair and find that what once was blond is now long and grey with metallic shimmering ends in the sunlight. I think I might have had it done at the salon like that, after William first went missing. Didn't I? I examine my hair to look for evidence of a dye job, search for a memory of going out and to the salon, but the memory, if it exists, is not there.

My breath feels constricted as I search through memory and though I find nothing there, it has brought his presence back into the house. The room is filled with him. I look down at the pigeon on my lap and begin to lightly stroke its downy neck. It rises toward the affection, presses into my fingers. Pigeons stare up at me from the floor or down at me from the counters and furniture and shelves. I open my mouth to call to them.

"Whoooo. Whoooo." I say. I clear my throat, and again with less tremor, "Whooooo. Whooooo."

***

Lily doesn't think about pigeons or husbands. She doesn't have the time. She rushes from the house, shoves her way hard through the birds' bodies, crushing a foot, crashing against an open wing as she rushes from the house, calling down the street for Amy.

"Amy," she shouts, looking down the road one way, then turning to do the same in the next.

When had she last seen her daughter? What did she look like? But her thoughts are blurry.

A hundred birds swoop above her, from side to side, following the line her body makes out on the soulless black tar. She has an image in her mind of a blond haired, blue-eyed girl. A girl that was quick to laugh, loud and riotous, like Lily used to be before. A spunky girl who loved to climb the maple trees in the park, swing from the top branch and make monkey noises and scare the daylights out of her mother while her father sat nearby and chortled.

"Like father, like daughter," he would say. Or, at least, she thinks he said, would say, had said.

Lily takes off running down the street in search of the daughter she's sure should be upstairs in bed but isn't. Her heart beats at a dangerous pace and though the air is frigid her body feels like its running through the desert tundra. She runs in the direction of her friend's house. Beth had been her best friend since high school, but after she married William, they drifted apart. That's a nice way to put it. It's more like they were wedged apart, incrementally. William was a toddler. He didn't like sharing. At first Lily thought it was sweet, flattering really. He wanted her all the time. It was passionate. It was romantic. Until it wasn't.

The grey bodies of pigeon's swoop through the wind above her, looking like a swarm, as she runs from one street to the next, across town. People stare but she has eyes only for the image in her mind of her missing daughter. The sun is blotted out by the storm of birds above her. They're like her own personal thunderhead. She reaches the light pink Victorian on the corner of 5th and Main, runs up the porch, and bangs on the door.

"Beth," she calls over and over. Pigeons flutter and perch around her, like an army, her own personal guard.

The door opens and Beth stands there, wiping her hands down with a hand towel. How old her friend's hands look, they're not baby soft smooth like she remembers. There are creases between fingers, knuckles bunched. Her green eyes are wide and she pushes the screen door open and the clatter of it reverberates in Lily's ears. Her face a startled mask of a person Lily used to know.

"Lily," she says, reaching out and grabbing her old friend's hands. "What is it? What's going on? Has William been found? Did he come back?"

Lily shakes her head, "No, no."

She feels confused, lost in the face and questions of her dear old friend. How does she know about William being gone? She turns her head to the side, away from the bright glare of her friend's wizened face. The pigeons sit around her, unblinking, and in their stares, she remembers why she's here, why she fled like a woman being pursued all the way across town.

"It's Amy." Lily starts, but her voice catches in her throat, like a hesitation. "I can't find Amy."

Lily looks up, expecting to see the earnest face of her friend, but instead she finds that Beth's body looks collapsed on itself, her face tilted down.

"Oh. Lil," she almost whispers. "Amy is gone. She's been gone. Don't you remember?"

Lily cocks her head to the right and the birds around her follow suit. A hundred birdlike heads on tilt.

"But I don't understand," Lily says. "Where did she go?"

Beth guides Lily over to her porch swing and Lily looks on as pigeons scoot over or fly up in the air to make room for them to sit. She blinks rapidly, waiting for Beth's response.

"Honey," she finally says, taking a deep breath in. "Lillian—" again, she pauses.

"What? What is it?"

"Amy was a still-born," at last she says.

She shakes her head rapidly in a no.

"No, I remember her blond hair. Her laughter, it was William's laugh, his stubbornness."

Tears streak Lily's face.

"I think," Beth weighs her words carefully, "that you are remembering the dream of your daughter." She rubs the tops of her friend's hands with her thumbs. "We buried Amy, in the Green Haven Cemetery, next to your parents."

Lily searches for the sound of her daughter's laugh but instead hears the crunch of a gravel road and the sound of her black boots crushing it under foot.

"No, but..." she tries to conjure the face of Amy, but now it's a granite slab.

She stares into the older face of her friend and she sees her younger friend, an image super-imposed over this one. Beth, her soft face and tender eyes. The feel of her delicate hand being crushed by the pressure of Lily's. She feels the weight of her stomach like she did that day, as if Amy were still inside there, waiting to take her first breath. The breath that she would never have.

She can see the gravestone with Amy's name on it and just the one date, standing so miniature next to the statuesque head stones of Lily's mother and father, towering over Amy's, shadowing it. She would never think miniature things were cute again. She placed the knitted booties on the overturned earth. The slippers. William wasn't there. He couldn't bear it.

Lily stands and moves away from Beth's body. Beth stands too, trying to close the distance, but Lily pulls from her again. She turns from her and races down the steps.

"I'm sorry," she calls over her shoulder, over the birds fluttering in the space between them, ready to fly. "I'm sorry. I shouldn't have come."

"No, Lil. It's okay," Beth says, shouting now, but Lily already can't hear her. Her mind is elsewhere. It is up in the air. It has taken flight.

***

You read somewhere that a pigeon appearing to you is a spiritual sign of divine truth. A pigeon appearance is said to mean you should pay attention. *A bunch of bullshit*, you think. Pay attention to what? The massive ocean frothing out the window? The empty space in your bed and how you're both devastated it's empty and relieved that he is gone? Pay attention to the way your mind feels fluttery and frantic.

You watch the young girl who ran by your house turn and run away. *Run far away*, you think. *Be free.* You were the young girl running.

There's a large pigeon sitting on your mailbox. Though now you know, or think you know, that it really isn't there. The sound of wings beats loudly behind you, and you turn around to see the birds take the shape of a man. They don't become the man; they just flutter in formation. They become the space of where William would be. The shape is undeniable. It is unfathomable that he is still here. Still with you. He was a ghost those last years he was alive, pacing the hallways of your house in the dark.

"I know it is you. Go away. Go away, Willy."

The pigeons shoot up into the sky as if frightened away by the sound of a bullet.

You watch them lift up into the world, leaving the ground, leaving you.

"No. Come back! Take me with you!"

Love is like that sometimes. When loves goes wrong it can be both something you can't stand to release and yet something you're dying to let go.

You squat down, William's boots pressing up in your knees. The pressure feels nice. It feels right. It feels sharp. Your body feels tight. It feels round. You feel expansive. You're expanding. You tilt your head, and your neck stretches, it feels elongated.

You think about all the other ways this story could go, could have gone, has been, never was. You feel a sort of buoyancy, a loosening in your bones. You push up through your joints to rise. You're no longer tethered to the ground.

Acknowledgments

Torpedo appeared in *Juked*.

Porcelain Ghosts appeared in *[PANK]*.

The Blue appeared in *New England College Magazine*.

Seeking Soul Mate at the Granada Theater appeared in *Parhelion Magazine*.

The Girl with the Dragonfly Wings appeared in *The Gateway Review*.

Grizzly appeared in *Gingerbread House*.

The Fisherman's Wife is forthcoming in *Cream Scene Carnival Magazine where Deer-Hearted and Pomegranate Seeds & the Hearts of Men have also appeared*.

Pigeon House first appeared in *Honey Literary Magazine*.

Thanks

First and foremost, thanks to Emily Perkovich. After a mishap with a shady press who accepted this manuscript and then ghosted me (not in a fun way like the ghosts in some of these stories) I was ready to call it quits, but Emily wouldn't let me. She took Pigeon House under her wing in the way she has done for me now on numerous occasions, and I will never be done being grateful for her.

Thanks to—in no particular order—Jordana, Ani, Andrea, Delilah, Brittany, Catherine, Becky, Paula (aka mom), Stacey, Dawn, Susan, Mazzy, Grandma Janice (long gone but not forgotten), Arianna, Blair (RIP), and all the hard-ass women who have come before us. I'm so lucky to have you all as a support network, to get to laugh and cry with you, to get to write stories for the ways in which we've been wronged and try to make it a little alright. I wouldn't survive or have survived parts of my life without you all.

Thanks to my NEC MFA family and mentors, who read and critiqued early versions of this collection. And thanks to the Spring Creek Trillium Project for the stay in the Spring Creek Cabin where I wrote Shiver, Tree Woman.

Thanks to my dad, Riff, and my brothers and cousins, my uncles Joshua and Karl, my sister's husband, Chris, and last but not least, my partner Andy who continues to show-up, even when I make it really hard. Dudes. I love you all. Thanks for being good guys (most of the time).

Mostly, I'm thankful for women, for their hearts, their anger, their magic, their resilience, their tough-as-nails exterior and cupcake interiors, their brilliant minds, their bomb bodies, their fire.